Murder at the Montrose Mansion

*A Mallory Beck Cozy
Culinary Caper (Book 5)*

Denise Jaden

Denise Jaden Books

Murder at the Montrose Mansion

There are plenty of things a girl wants to do on her sixteenth birthday. Clearing a family member from suspicion of murder isn't one of them.

Amber is finally turning sixteen, and Mallory is determined to make the day perfect, baking her everything from brioche to pink lemonade cupcakes for the party her mom is throwing her. Their favorite Honeysuckle Grove detective, Alex Martinez, will be in attendance, too, at least until he gets called away to investigate a recently discovered death involving foul play.

When Amber's last name is the only clue given as to what they might find at the nearby crime scene, Alex and Mallory decide they might have to keep this one quiet or Amber's sixteenth birthday will be anything but sweet.

Join my mystery readers' newsletter today!

Sign up now, and you'll get access to a special mystery as well as bonus epilogues to accompany this series—an exclusive bonus for newsletter subscribers.
In addition, you'll be the first to hear about new releases and sales, and receive special excerpts and behind-the-scenes bonuses. Visit the link below to sign up and receive your first bonus epilogue:

https://www.subscribepage.com/mysterysignup

Chapter One

Nothing says "party time" better than three dozen pink lemonade cupcakes.

I balanced my tiered cupcake holder on the hood of Alex's 90s Toyota to make sure they hadn't been jostled too much *en route*.

"You're sure you want to do that here?" Alex raised an eyebrow at me, looking very much like the boy I'd had an unrelenting crush on in the seventh grade.

After a recent storm, I was almost knee-deep in snow, in a dress made for warmer weather, worried about the state of my baking. It *was* ridiculous. I offered up the only excuse I had. "If food is all I can contribute to my best friend's sixteenth birthday, I'm going to make it amazing."

Alex snickered and lifted the Rubbermaid container with the rest of my prepared food from the backseat. "I thought I was your best friend."

I blushed, despite the frigid air. Alex would count as something akin to my best friend if my feelings for him weren't so...complicated.

"Besides, when has your food *not* been amazing?"

I blushed harder. I had approached Amber's mom, Helen Montrose, almost a month ago to check and see if it was okay if I threw Amber a small birthday celebration. Helen had been emerging from her fog of grief over her husband's death at the time and trying to make up for emotionally abandoning her children in the months prior. She countered by saying that her mother should really be the one to throw her a sweet-sixteen party.

I had my reservations. Helen Montrose still had days where she couldn't get herself out of bed, and from what Amber told me, she wouldn't have a clue who to invite.

At the same time, my concerns were twofold. I wanted the best for Amber, of course, but I also didn't want her mother turning around and telling her that she should find a best friend her own age—not some twenty-eight-year-old widow who liked to solve murder investigations in her spare time.

So, for the most part, I had pasted on a smile and an agreeable attitude, and encouraged Helen Montrose to take the helm of Amber's party. I only offered a handful of suggestions for the invitation list and begged that I could contribute some food.

I followed Alex up the walkway to the front door of the Montrose mansion. Snow had leaked down the sides of my boots—Alex was right; the hood of his car had not been the best place to rearrange cupcakes—and I was already shivering from the thin purple dress I'd selected. I hoped this was all simply a bad start to a good day.

"You ready?" Alex asked me before pressing on the doorbell. It was as if he knew I needed a minute to breathe and reapply my smile.

I nodded. "You bet."

The door opened in front of us, and a very put-together Helen Montrose stood on the other side, all bouffant hairstyle and plastic grin. Amber's mother truly must have an on/off switch. But I couldn't concentrate on any of that because with the opening of the door, an overhang let go of a foot of snow right on top of my head.

It dripped down my face and inside my coat. With a startled gasp, I arched my back at the icy droplets making their way down my neck. The insides of my boots now held enough of the white stuff to start a snowball fight.

Somehow, I saved the cupcakes.

"Oh, dear!" Helen said. "Let me help." But she didn't make any move forward to do so.

"Oh, Mal…" Alex brushed the snow from my head and the back of my coat, but I could tell he was trying not to giggle. Although, who was I kidding? I would've done the same if it had happened to him.

"Just…take the cupcakes!" I said to both of

them.

This Helen Montrose could handle. She reached out for my tray, and I used both my newly free hands to wipe the snow and my soaked hair away from my face.

"Is that Mallory—?" Amber's words were cut off when she came around her mother and saw my snow-soaked appearance. She, unlike Alex, didn't hold back her laugher. I tilted my head and raised my eyebrows until she could collect herself. "Come up to my room," she said when she could overcome her amusement. "I'll get you something dry to wear."

I'd only been in Amber's bedroom one time, on the very first day I met her—when I'd arrived to deliver a casserole on behalf of the church, right in the middle of her father's wake. That day, it had also been a Sunday afternoon, but so much else had changed for both of us.

We had become much closer since then, and it seemed odd to me when I followed her into her pin-neat pink room that she spent most of her nights here, in a place I barely knew.

She threw a pair of leggings and one of her oversized hoodies onto the bed. "These should fit."

I shrugged out of my coat and let out a groan. "But I wore purple, just for you."

Purple was Amber's current favorite color. I'd decorated the cupcakes and cheesecake bites in purple butterflies and sprinkles for exactly that reason.

"Well, if it's just for me, then you're in luck because I don't care." She dug her fists into the sides of her waist, as if daring me to argue. She wore one of her own oversized hoodies. I shouldn't have been surprised, as most of her wardrobe was made up of hoodies with big statements. This one was royal blue and read: MY LIFE IS BASED ON A TRUE STORY. "I'll leave you to change. You can meet *us* downstairs."

She rolled her eyes on that last bit, so as she shut the door behind her, I wondered what the "us" was I might find down in her living room.

Chapter Two

When I'd been planning to have my own party for Amber, I'd mentally made a guest list, a menu, and come up with a few fun ideas for entertainment, too. When Helen Montrose decided it was the mother's job to hold the sweet-sixteen party, I put the rest out of my mind. At least until now.

I left Amber's bedroom feeling much frumpier than I had when I'd arrived. Truth be told, I'd wanted to look nice for myself as well, and maybe even a tiny bit for Alex. But too late for any of that.

When I reached the top of the stairs, a voice from inside another bedroom surprised me. "You're not hiding up here again, are you, sis?" The door to the room swung open to reveal Amber's older brother, Seth. "Oh." Seth looked me up and down for a few long seconds, processing that I wasn't Amber. He may have also been processing me in her clothes. The bright red hoodie she'd left on the bed for me read: THIS IS NOT A DRILL and included a picture of a hammer.

"I...um...the snow out your front door dumped on me. I had to change," I explained. I felt like I was forever explaining myself to Amber's mother and brother because why *would* a twenty-eight-year-old woman take such a strong interest in a fifteen-year-old?

Sixteen-year-old.

In truth, Amber had been exactly what I'd needed after my husband died and I'd had trouble climbing out of my own pit of grief. I think I'd been what she needed after her dad's death, too. It was kismet, and now we had a lot of fun together cooking the nights away, and solving crimes whenever Alex allowed us to help with his investigations.

Seth nodded and looked like he was about to laugh as well about my misfortune, but he didn't. "I've looked up at that overhang a few times, wondering when it was going to dump."

But you never thought to fix it? I held back the words before saying them. Seth and Amber had pretty much been parenting themselves since their dad died six months ago. I wasn't about to blame either one of them for any neglect of the house.

"No worries. It's only water," I said instead. *Cold* water, but still. "Amber's been hiding away? From what?"

Seth let out one laugh and motioned to the stairs. "See for yourself."

Now I was really curious. "You're not joining us?"

Seth and Amber had become protectively close to one another in recent months. It surprised me if he wasn't going to take part in her birthday party.

He laughed again and simply said, "Later," before closing the door between us.

The stairway of the mansion led into the dining room, where I found Alex holding a platter of deviled eggs and looking lost about where to put it. Poor guy had been left on his own for food duty.

I rushed over. "Here, let me take that." I placed the platter in an open space on the table. "I'm sorry you got left with all of this." As I spoke, I rearranged platters on the table so that the savory items were at one end with the sweet treats on the other. Then I reached for the next tray—brioche buns—from my Rubbermaid bin.

"Actually, I was taking my time in here." Alex glanced over his shoulder toward the living room where some soft background music streamed through, but not much else.

"You're trying to escape Amber's party, too? Why? What's wrong with it?"

Alex shrugged one shoulder, but didn't answer. Clearly, it was up to me to see where on earth Helen Montrose had gone wrong.

I reached for the platter of deviled eggs, along with a stack of napkins, pasted on my most professional catering smile, and marched for the door.

The Montrose's living room boasted expensive hardwood furniture and knickknacks. Even the first time I'd been in here, six months ago at Dan Montrose's wake, it had felt like a room that sat untouched most of the time. With a dozen teenagers sprinkled around the room, I should have felt an immediate worry for the costly décor, but instead, I felt instant dread for another reason.

Amber didn't have teenage friends. She'd been an outcast at school even before her dad died, and after his death, no one knew what to say to her. She'd always been a girl who spoke her mind and had plenty of smart and sarcastic remarks. "Too smart for her own good" was a way Alex often described her.

So what were all of these schoolmates doing here?

I took in a deep breath and let it out slowly with my understanding. Helen Montrose had ignored my list of older church friends who Amber at least liked and decided she knew best. She had invited a slew of classmates from the local high school who Amber never spoke to.

Meanwhile, Amber, at her own birthday party, sat in a nearby armchair, legs slung over the side, flipping through a magazine and paying little attention to the rest of the people in the room.

It seemed as though Mrs. Montrose had not only invited a slew of people who weren't friendly with Amber, but they didn't even seem friendly with each other.

Amber's mother whisked in from another door, carrying a large square black speaker with a handle. "Who's ready for karaoke?"

She had to be kidding. With her plastic smile, though, she didn't seem to take in the awkwardness in the room.

"Actually, we were about to have some food," I announced and headed straight for the one person in the room I recognized. Marcy Ralston had been Amber's prime competitor in a recent cooking contest at the school. While they may not have liked each other, at least they had mutual respect. "Would you like a deviled egg? They're my own special recipe."

Marcy was tucked as far to one side of a loveseat as she could be, clearly not friends with the purple-haired girl on the other end. I wondered if Helen Montrose had simply invited the purple-haired girl because she thought her daughter would like her based on hair color.

Marcy looked thankful at the deviled egg offer. She helped herself to a napkin from my hand and then a half egg. "Better than karaoke," she murmured.

"Your mom owns a local bakery, right?" I asked. Because no one else in the room was speaking, my voice seemed extra loud. Helen Montrose had ignored my comment about the food and stooped behind a brocade couch to reach for an electrical outlet.

Marcy nodded. "Karen's Bake Shop."

"I don't think I've tried that one. What's your favorite menu item? I'll have to stop by." I actually had been by there and the two other bakeries in town. Karen's Bake Shop was my favorite with a memorable apple pie. Regardless, my conversation starter had the desired effect and other girls from around the room started murmuring to one another. The thing I'd learned about teenagers in the last six months was that you needed a discreet ice breaker to get them talking. In my experience, the topic of tasty food usually worked.

When the purple-haired girl asked Marcy, "Your mom owns that place?" I left them to discuss and moved along to my next victim, a girl chewing gum so violently, I'd swear she must have a jaw condition.

Before long, I'd covered most of the room, and my tray was empty. At least more people in the room had started talking. An untouched plate of store-bought cookies and cupcakes sat in the middle of a coffee table. I wondered if one of these girls had brought them or if that was Helen Montrose's contribution to the food.

When I ducked back into the dining room, ready to give Alex a piece of my mind for continuing to hide out, I found him on his cell phone. He had his back to me and didn't see me as I placed the empty egg platter down and reached for my cupcake tree. I considered putting the candles I'd brought into it, but the longer I took in here, the more I suspected all conversation in the other room would cease once again. Besides, this didn't seem like a happy-birthday-singing crowd.

If only Helen had invited Sasha and Donna and Denean from the church, like I'd suggested. She had started off well in trying to reconnect with her daughter but was obviously still struggling. That, or she was still uncomfortable having people from the church asking too many questions.

"What do you mean, you arrested him?" Alex hissed into his phone. He must have been on the line with his partner, Mickey Bradley. If Detective Bradley wasn't botching a case, he was making an arrest with little-to-no evidence. I felt bad for Alex, being paired with the worst detective on the force, especially when there were other police departments that would treat him much better. "How do you know this Ben Montrose is responsible for her death?"

My hand stopped on the cupcake I'd been adjusting. Did he just say Ben Montrose? The last name held familiarity, of course, but it was more than that. Back when I'd been helping to investigate Amber's dad's death, I'd heard of an uncle named Ben Montrose at the will reading.

Alex turned with his mouth ajar, about to say more, but stopped when he saw me. "Listen, Mickey, I've got to go. Please don't arrest anyone else until I get there." He hung up and stared at me for a long moment.

"Mickey arrested Amber's uncle?" I whispered. The people in the living room didn't need to hear about this, least of all Amber. "Who died?"

Alex nodded. "I'm pretty sure it's a mistake, but I have to get over to the property right away before Detective Bradley arrests the whole block. Can you make an excuse for me?"

"What does Mickey think he did?" It wasn't as though I wouldn't cover for Alex with Amber. If her uncle had somehow *actually* been involved in someone's death, the last thing I wanted was for her to hear about it during her birthday party—especially with teenagers who already didn't like her lining the room. But I'd been working with Alex for long enough that when he was working on a case, I had to know about it. Or, at least, I had to ask.

Alex took in a big breath and let it out in a sigh, which seemed ominous somehow. "There was a tiger attack on his property."

"And this is somehow his fault? Was it a wild tiger? Is there a zoo nearby or something that it escaped from? Did it wander into his yard?"

Alex shook his head solemnly, which made me catch my breath. But before he could say more, Seth made his way down the stairs from his bedroom.

"What's this about a wild tiger?" Seth raised an auburn eyebrow, which made him look a lot like his sister.

"Not wild, no," Alex said to Seth but kept his eyes on me. Everything about his unwavering gaze told me this was serious.

"My Uncle Ben has a pet tiger." By Seth's light tone, I suspected he hadn't caught on to Alex's concern, and I didn't want him to, nor did I want him to hear how much this had to do with his Uncle Ben, for fear it might get back to Amber.

"I didn't know people kept tigers as pets." I

13

forced lightness into my voice. "But you know who the real tigers are? Those silent teenage girls in your front room. Any chance you want to help me loosen things up out there?" Without waiting for an answer, I turned Seth toward the door to the front room and guided him toward it.

Before it swung shut behind us, I waved a hand back at Alex, encouraging him to go.

Seth had a surprising amount of influence over the teenage girls in his living room and clearly cared for his sister because I couldn't have seen him volunteering to sing karaoke with girls two years younger than him any other time.

He invited Marcy Ralston to sing with him first, and that seemed to loosen everyone up. Marcy's voice was at least as good as her baking, which was saying a lot. Seth not so much, but the girls in the room gazed at him as though his voice was soaked in butter.

Once the karaoke party was underway, Helen Montrose disappeared through the door to the dining room and, I suspected, upstairs to her bedroom.

By the time Seth and Marcy finished singing a duet version of "Eye of the Tiger," half a dozen girls were swooning and begging Seth to sing with them next.

None of the girls had any time for Amber, but from the looks of her flipping through her third magazine, I doubted she cared. By the fourth duet, I was getting antsy about whatever Alex might have found out about Amber's uncle and snuck out to the bathroom.

Once I had the door closed behind me, I perched on the closed toilet, pulled out my cell phone, and navigated to Alex's number. He didn't pick up until the fourth ring, which told me he was busy, but I couldn't seem to bring myself to leave him alone.

"What's going on there? Was Mickey wrong to arrest Ben Montrose? Was someone really killed?"

Alex, as usual, didn't seem bothered by my slew of questions, even if it bothered me that I was distracting him from his work. "Unfortunately, yes. There's been a death on the property, and Mickey might be right this time in arresting the owner of the tiger for gross negligence and assault."

"Oh, no. He attacked the person that was killed?"

"No, the attack was actually on a neighbor who was trying to shoot at his tiger." Alex covered his mouthpiece and called a directive, probably to the forensics team.

"And you're at the property now investigating?" I asked as soon as he was back on the line. A knock sounded at the bathroom door, so I dropped my voice. "When will you know more?"

"I have no idea. Forensics was about to leave by the time I arrived, which is ridiculous, but I guess Mickey told them to give the place a once-over and that would be enough. Sometimes I don't know what to do with the neglect on this force. I insisted they stay and conduct a thorough investigation, as a woman had lost her life today."

"Who was the woman?" I whispered. When another knock sounded, I flushed the toilet, under the pretense of using the bathroom for its intended purpose.

"Listen, I've got to run, but why don't you get over here when the party is done and you can get away without raising Amber's suspicions." He rattled off the address of the other Montrose mansion, and I made a note of it on the notepad in my purse.

"Sure thing. I'll get there as soon as I can sneak away." I ran the water as he hung up and then reached for the door. I stopped with my mouth open at Amber on the other side, scowling with her arms crossed.

"And here I thought you were creating a diversion to get *me* out of there, but instead, you were going to ditch me and leave me in the brood of vipers by myself?" Amber had a habit of being dramatic.

"I wasn't ditching you! I was coming right back."

"While Alex is off on an investigation?" She raised a Seth-like eyebrow in disbelief.

She made it sound as though I never let Alex work alone. "I was going to head over there *after* your party."

"You mean *that* party?" She motioned over

her shoulder and toward the living room, where a bad duet version of "Sweet Caroline" streamed our way. "You realize the best gift you could give me for my birthday would be to get me out of here and over to whatever investigation pulled Detective Martinez away."

It wasn't that I didn't want to do just that. But this was her uncle we were talking about, and the girl had lost her father only six months ago. "But your mom planned this and everything."

"Right, and she *clearly* spent a lot of time thinking about what I would like." Amber didn't let me argue this point, not that I could. "And she's *for sure* not upstairs drugging herself up for the rest of the day right this second."

The way she said it so plainly made me feel worse for her than I had already. "At least your mom has been trying lately." Amber's tired look made me try another tactic. "And Seth…" Even this argument held zero conviction.

"Seth owes me for forgetting to pick me up from school on that day it was practically a blizzard out." Amber had called me that day, so it wasn't as though she'd had to walk home in the "near-blizzard," though I was sure she'd made her brother think she had.

"You really want to leave in the middle of your own party?"

Her eyebrow raised higher, and she didn't have to respond to this weaker-than-weak rebuttal.

I was more than happy to get her out of here. More than happy to have her help with an investigation. And she truly was able to have perspective over family faults more than anyone I knew.

Still, I didn't know whether or not I was making a mistake when I opened my mouth to say, "But, Amber, it has something to do with your uncle."

Chapter Three

"Uncle Ben?" Amber furrowed her brow. When I didn't respond right away, she filled in the missing information herself. "He's my only uncle who's local. It must be him."

My smart sixteen-year-old sleuth friend was in a habit of deducing clues before Alex or I could get around to fully explaining all the known information.

"Yes, it's your Uncle Ben." Any other time, I may have made a crack about her uncle being named after a relative of Spiderman, but now was not the time. "I don't know much. Only that it has to do with his pet tiger."

Amber rolled her eyes. "Me and Mom have told him a thousand times that Boots wasn't happy there. He got out, didn't he?"

I shrugged. "I don't know the details, only that he attacked a woman earlier today."

"Is she okay?" Without waiting for my answer, Amber led the way through a back hallway, into the kitchen, and then to her mudroom. It seemed we were sneaking out the back door.

"No," I said, slipping my feet into the snow

boots Amber set in front of me. For the first time today, I was glad to be in leggings and a hoodie— and then one of Amber's warm snow jackets. "She's not."

Thankfully, Amber knew what I meant without me having to explain further. "And this is somehow Uncle Ben's fault?" she guessed. "Did he leave the cage open?" Even as she asked this question, she looked like she would find this hard to believe.

"I have no idea," I said. As she reached for the door, I stopped her. "Hang on. How are we going to get there? I came here with Alex."

Most problems in Amber's world were only fun diversions. She took about three seconds to think this over and then grabbed a set of keys off a hook by the door. "I guess I'm going to owe Seth for two things this time."

I hadn't driven a standard transmission vehicle since I'd first taken driver's ed back in high school. I didn't feel great about driving Seth's bright blue Corvette in the snow either, especially since he'd just recently gotten it running, but it turned out, it handled a lot better than my Prius. Besides, I wanted to get to Alex's investigation badly enough that I was willing to put my reservations aside.

The other Montrose mansion was several miles away on the other side of Honeysuckle Grove in the flats. Even though I had the address, Amber knew the directions well enough that I didn't need my phone's GPS.

"So all you know is that Mickey Mouse arrested my Uncle Ben after Boots attacked some woman on his property?"

Alex had been the first to nickname his incompetent partner, Detective Mickey Bradley, as Mickey Mouse. There was, however, nothing playful about the name when Amber used it.

Still, Detective Bradley may not have been wrong or incompetent on this particular occasion.

"I think he was brought in on gross negligence," I told her as I turned onto a road that led outside the town limits.

"Sounds like he left the gate open, but Uncle Ben is careful when it comes to Boots. That tiger is his pride and joy, practically like a son. He's the reason my aunt and uncle split up—because he loved that big cat more than he loved her." She harrumphed. "I could almost understand if it was a nice kitty like Hunch, but he's totally not nice to anyone, even to Uncle Ben."

My late husband's cat, Hunch, was far from being a *nice* kitty, at least to anyone other than Amber, but I chose to stay focused on the topic at hand. "Has Boots ever attacked anyone before this?"

"Not really attacked, no. But he jumps at the fence if he's in a bad mood or hasn't eaten in a while. A couple of years ago, a neighbor's rabbit got out of its cage and wandered too close. Boots bit him through the fence, and the rabbit bled out before it could get away. Uncle Ben *bragged* about that for months. He likes to hold back his food leading up to the weekend and then throw a couple of live chickens in the cage to keep his hunting instincts alive. Me and Mom stopped visiting because Boots is just so aggressive. Seth still thinks the tiger is cool, but I'm convinced that Boots is actually going crazy because he doesn't have enough room to roam. Did you know a male Siberian tiger is supposed to have forty square miles if you keep them in captivity? They're clearly not meant to be pets."

I turned onto the street where, if I couldn't pick out the Montrose mansion by its gigantic size, I'd pick it out by the police cars lining the street in front of it. It was like the crown jewel, sitting in the midst of suburbia. All the surrounding houses were about the size of mine or smaller, nothing fancy or extravagant. The Montrose mansion, on the other hand, was decorated with two-story cement columns out front, a four-car garage, and an angled fence on either side that seemed to widen the backyard.

That must be where he kept Boots, his tiger.

I found a spot to pull in between two police cars. "Is keeping a tiger as a pet even legal?"

Amber shrugged. "In West Virginia, it used to be. I think Uncle Ben got a permit for Boots a few years ago before the laws changed. Mom joined a local animal rights association and was partially responsible for changing the laws. That put some tension between our family and his. People like Uncle Ben will fight tooth and nail to keep their rights, but the animal rights association was pretty angry that his permit wasn't revoked."

"Did your mom drop out of the association after your dad died?" I usually held back any outright questions about how her dad's death had affected her family, but when focused on a new investigation, the question just came out.

Amber also seemed to have less discomfort with the subject as we worked through the backstory of a case. "Nah, she quit that one a couple of years ago. She found another cause to focus on. I think she just felt old working with the young couple that made up the rest of the committee. Mom's more of a bureaucrat—she likes to aim her ammunition at the government systems, while Bruce and Lynda, they liked to get out there and get their hands dirty."

"Huh. Well, I can't imagine there's too much to investigate here, if someone was killed because the tiger wasn't properly contained. I guess the only question is how a judge will feel about the situation."

"Why do you think Detective Martinez is still here, then?"

That was a good question. "Why don't we go and find out."

Unlike Amber's mansion, which was located on a hillside overlooking Honeysuckle Grove with mansions close on either side, Ben Montrose seemed to have the only large house and lot on the block. Still, it was no forty miles' worth of tiger-roaming land. Twenty-foot-high barrier walls lined the property, but Amber knew exactly where to go to find a gate to let us in. The cedar wooden gate looked as if the areas around the latch were covered in black fingerprint dust. That was curious. It had been left ajar, and when we walked through it, there was more fingerprint dust on the other side.

"Wait, we're not going to find an agitated tiger on the other side of this gate, right?" I asked nervously.

Amber laughed. "Nope. Boots has a separate enclosure. If he was left to roam the whole yard, there's no way Uncle Ben would've gotten a permit to keep him."

That made sense, but I still felt anxious as I led the way through the gate. Even if I was about to face up against a rabid wild animal, there was no way I'd let Amber go first.

Noises sounded immediately through the gate. Voices yelled to one another about "code number such-and-such" and "bagging item so-and-so." I recognized Alex's voice when he called out, "And cordon off this patch of snow. I want to try and decipher some footprints."

"Footprints?" Amber asked from behind me. "Why do they need footprints and fingerprints if they've got my uncle for gross negligence? Do they think someone else might have opened the cage?" I shrugged from in front of her as we made our way along the plowed path at the side of the mansion. She didn't wait for me to come up with any kind of an answer and just went on with her theories. "I wonder if it was Bruce and Lynda. According to my mom, they do stuff like this all the time."

"The local animal rights association lets exotic animals out in town, no matter the consequences?" I found that hard to believe.

"I think they'd usually stay nearby with a tranquilizer gun. It's their way of proving danger and getting permits revoked." Amber shrugged. "Besides, we're not exactly in town."

I held my tongue from arguing that we weren't exactly *outside* of town either, especially when a male tiger had a forty-mile roaming radius. It didn't seem very responsible of the animal rights folks to me, but maybe Amber was right. It might get her uncle off the hook if Alex could prove it, anyway.

We rounded the corner into a wide, open backyard and saw half a dozen forensics officers in various states of evidence gathering. Through a sliding glass door, others moved around inside.

"Why do you think they're in the house?" Amber asked as I thought it. Before I could answer, Alex spotted us and came right over.

"I'm glad you two are here." He stopped and turned to Amber. "Wait, what about your party?"

"You mean the teenybopper-karaoke-fest my mother planned for all the people who don't like me?"

Alex raised an eyebrow in response. I could have argued that after Seth sang a song with each of them and gave their sophomore selves a little senior male attention, they may have had a better attitude toward his sister, but there were more important matters at hand.

"What have you discovered?" I dropped my voice. "Was Detective Bradley right in arresting Ben Montrose?" I kept my eyes from Amber's, wondering if her uncle's fate might start to bother her more once she was in the thick of the situation.

"I wish I knew. I've been finding a lot of conflicting evidence." He shook his head.

"Such as?" Amber pushed.

"We've lifted some fingerprints, which appear to be from narrow hands, from the rear side of the back gate and larger ones from the front side."

"And...?" I didn't get why Alex thought this was important, unless Amber was correct and someone like the animal rights people had been here to tamper with the tiger's enclosure.

"And we couldn't find prints anywhere else on any doors to the house or even on the keypad of the tiger enclosure."

"So someone else tampered with the keypad and let Boots out?" Amber guessed. "And not the person who was killed?"

Alex shook his head. "The outer gate to the tiger cage was sealed shut when the police arrived. The inner gate was open with the woman partially inside. The strange part is that the keypad and handle to the gate, as well as all the knobs and handles to the house, seem to have been wiped clean with a solvent of some kind. Forensics has taken a sample to look into it, but they suspect it's an acetone-based solvent."

"Like nail polish remover?" I asked. My mind immediately returned to the animal rights activists, Bruce and Lynda. I wondered if Lynda kept nail polish remover wipes in her purse.

Alex went on with the rest of what he'd uncovered. "When the police found Ben Montrose, he was in a tussle with a neighbor, a Mr. Cliff Barber." As Alex spoke, he moved toward the middle of the large yard where a small square had been marked off with crime scene tape. Much of the ground within the square was visible, as the snow had been haphazardly cleared aside through the tussle.

"Did this neighbor open the tiger pen?" I asked, looking at the distance between the square and the large chain-link fence that I had to assume housed a tiger, although one was not visible at the moment. The fence stretched at least a hundred feet in the distance and covered a good stretch of land, but nowhere near forty miles. Tall spindly trees stretched high above the height of the fence, and there was a large stone-carved area toward the far side of the enclosure with a stone doorway at the back. The stone door was open, so I had to assume that Boots the tiger had disappeared somewhere within it. The rest of the cage was all wide, open space, visible from where I stood.

The altercation between Ben and his neighbor only happened maybe forty feet from the fence, close to a small barn that, from the clucking within, seemed to house chickens. I couldn't imagine the neighbor thinking he could open the tiger enclosure and get away in time, especially once he was tackled.

But Alex flipped through pages of a file folder in his hands, reading. "Apparently, the neighbor came over because he heard concerning noises from the yard. When he found that Ben Montrose wasn't home, he assumed a problem with the tiger and raced to the backyard with his gun. He saw a woman getting attacked in the tiger cage and pulled his gun to get the tiger to stop. Ben Montrose came home right then and tackled the neighbor before he could shoot at the tiger."

I squinted. "So why was Ben Montrose arrested?"

"The neighbor wasn't in great shape when Mickey arrived. Two cops had pulled the men apart after a phone call from another neighbor who heard a gunshot. Mickey called an ambulance for the neighbor, but Ben barely had a scratch on him."

"I thought nobody shot Boots?" Amber's gaze drifted back and forth over the tiger enclosure.

"Boots is the name of the tiger," I explained to Alex.

He nodded. "Nobody shot the tiger, but through the scuffle between the two men, the gun went off. When Mickey arrived, Cliff, the neighbor, was practically unconscious, but he got out the words, 'I just wanted to help,' as they took him away in the ambulance."

I took in a big breath and heaved it out. It made sense, then, why Ben Montrose would have been arrested. Even Amber said, "Yup. That's Uncle Ben, protecting his cat at all costs."

I shushed her, as that kind of character witness wouldn't be helpful to her uncle's case.

"I only meant he wouldn't want Boots shot." Amber didn't like to misspeak, which was clear in her tone.

Alex, who always seemed to know how to divert Amber from any discomfort, changed the subject. "When was the last time you visited your uncle's house?"

Amber shrugged. "Probably around March. He'd gotten an antique dining table he wanted to show off. Dad had talked Mom into it because she didn't want to be anywhere near a tiger in captivity."

"Did your uncle acquire his tiger as an adult?" Alex made a note when Amber confirmed this. "And you were inside the house at the time of your last visit?" Amber nodded about this as well. Alex beckoned a uniform-clad officer toward him. When the officer got close, he said, "Officer Krause, will you please accompany Miss Montrose inside the house and make a note of anything she recognizes as out of place?"

Before Officer Krause could offer his agreement, Amber marched toward the sliding glass door, leading the way.

"Inside?" I asked as soon as they were out of earshot. If Amber hadn't been here in almost a year, I couldn't imagine her being of much help. "Because of the wiped-off handles and door-knobs?"

Alex nodded. "Partially, yes. Ben Montrose knew the victim of the tiger attack, and she appeared to have gone inside first."

I stared at Alex as he left a dramatic pause.

"She was his girlfriend. They'd only been dating a month, but she had been to his house several times and knew the combination to the front door lock."

"But her fingerprints weren't on it?" I asked.

Alex shook his head. "No one's were. Not even Ben's."

That was more than curious. "Did she also know the passcode to the tiger enclosure?" I glanced over to the tall gate of metal bars.

Alex led the way closer and pointed to a piece of cardstock taped above a keypad. In black marker, it read: 84239. "It's written right above the lockbox for anyone to use."

"So Ben Montrose claims his girlfriend just wandered in there, knowing there was a tiger inside?" Were we talking about another murder case here? I didn't want to believe that, and my mind returned to the animal rights activists. "Or do you think someone planned to set it free?"

"We don't know yet, but there's no evidence of tampering with the lock and the outer door to the enclosure was clicked shut with her inside when police arrived."

I looked toward the inner gate, made of the same type of metal bars, which now sat wide open. The victim's body had been covered with a sheet, but blood marked the snowy ground. Shreds of what looked like carpet were also strewn around the inside the enclosure as well as between the two gates.

"Ben claimed he didn't open or shut either of the gates in the tiger enclosure today. There was evidence of water on the floors throughout the house. It indicates that either the victim, Stella Havenshack, or Ben Montrose himself trekked through the house in wet boots before arriving in the backyard. It looked as though it could have been more than one set of boots, but forensics is currently looking into that."

My heart stopped and I held my breath as a figure appeared through the rear stone door within the tiger enclosure. But I let out my breath when I registered that it wasn't a tiger. It was a heavyset man who wore a suit under his wool overcoat.

What was a businessman doing in the tiger enclosure? "Is he another detective?"

Alex shook his head. "That's Carson Kroeger from the Honeysuckle Grove Department of Agriculture. We called him in to subdue the tiger. I figured he would have taken him away, revoked Ben's permit on the spot, maybe even put the animal down, but he said the tiger is endangered and there would be a lot of red tape involved before any of that would happen."

Mr. Kroeger hit a silver pad along the stone wall I hadn't seen, and the stone door slid closed. Then he walked toward us and through both gates after Alex punched in the code to open the outer one. He held a long silver pole with what looked like the remains of a steak on a hook at one end. Without cleaning it off, he leaned it in the corner of the small four-foot square space between the gates. "The tiger's sedated and sequestered. Feel free to let your team in to do their job and give me a call when you're done."

"You're going to make sure the tiger isn't going to be a danger to anyone else?" Alex asked with narrowed eyes.

The businessman actually laughed at this suggestion. "This tiger isn't going to be a danger to anyone as long as they don't wander into this here cage while he's awake." Before Alex could respond, he added, "This animal can't be held responsible for an ignorant human." He pushed past me and Alex, taking one last glance into the enclosure before nodding to Alex and saying, "Good day, detective."

I watched him go, hardly believing he had so quickly blamed the victim of this attack *and* made light of it. "You called that guy in?" I asked Alex.

He raised his eyebrows, also watching Mr.

Kroeger round the corner out of the Montrose backyard. "I called the Department of Agriculture and asked them to send whoever would deal with a situation like this. Apparently, Mr. Kroeger is in charge of all animal permits in the municipality, so it came down to him."

I couldn't say there was anything suspicious about the man, per se, but there was certainly something unlikeable about his response.

I shook it off and got back to the details at hand. "Do you think the victim could have gone in by her free will and for some reason shut the outer door behind her?" My brow furrowed as I imagined an animal rights activist trying to simply tempt the tiger or lead him out of his enclosure. Perhaps this Stella Havenshack had joined forces with Bruce and Lynda from the animal rights association, and that's why she'd started dating Ben Montrose. Still, I couldn't imagine someone purposely making that move and putting her own life in danger.

"The motive doesn't make a lot of sense at this point. Plus, there must be someone else involved who would have removed any trace of fingerprints *after* she was inside the enclosure."

"Amber and I were talking on the way over about the local animal rights activists, and how angered they were at Ben keeping a tiger in a space that definitely wasn't big enough for a male tiger. Do you think they could be involved somehow?"

Alex took in a breath and let it out in a sigh,

pondering this. "It's definitely a thought. I'll contact the local organization as soon as I have a moment. Or maybe I'll have to get Mickey on it," he murmured as an afterthought.

I hoped it wouldn't come to that, as his partner, Detective Mickey Bradley, had a habit of missing crucial information or making quick, unwarranted arrests.

"I wanted to get Amber out of here before she got any closer. They've covered the body, but the scene still isn't pretty."

In truth, Amber could probably handle the gory details better than I could. She certainly had no problem talking about them. But somehow, in all of the murder investigations we'd helped with so far, she hadn't seen much gore.

We moved along the outside of the fence, and I sucked in another quick breath. While there wasn't a lot of blood, there was enough of it, in enough different visible places within the enclosure that I could imagine a full-size tiger whipping a woman around to stop her struggle.

We stood staring into the enclosure, looking for anything we might have missed. "Is this another murder?" I had to ask.

Alex sucked in a big breath and let it out slowly. "Let's hope we find something here today that helps us figure that out."

Chapter Four

We spent a long day in the Montrose yard, trying to come up with evidence or motives, but there wasn't a lot to be found.

Stella Havenshack hadn't left a single fingerprint on or in the tiger enclosure or the house.

"I asked forensics to rush the test on the solvent used to wipe the fingerprints clean. It could be a household cleaner, or like you suggested, it could be a nail polish remover." Alex sat at my kitchen table later that night. It was where we talked over most of the crimes he let me help investigate. "But I'm starting to think Mickey didn't jump the gun this one time in arresting Ben."

Amber had had to go home, so we could discuss this freely without concern of how protective she might feel about her uncle. Amber's mother had been furious when she woke up from her extended nap and found I'd absconded with her daughter. Seth had smoothed things over to some degree and even given Amber's partygoers a pretty great time, but Amber owed him a big favor for it, and Helen Montrose had texted me, saying she really didn't appreciate my interference this afternoon and that she thought it best if Amber and I took a break from seeing each other.

The idea of losing my best friend was enough to make me physically nauseous. I'd wanted to text her back, but Amber suggested I wait a day to let her mom calm down. I was doing all I could to put the situation out of my mind by focusing on the case.

"You think Ben could have pushed her into the tiger enclosure and then wiped his prints clean?" I asked Alex

"From Mickey's notes, it seemed Ben was solely concerned for his tiger. But perhaps his relationship with Stella hadn't been a match made in heaven." Alex turned his cell phone over and over in his hands, a nervous tick he had when he was deep in thought.

"So how do we prove that?" I snapped my mouth shut, not knowing why I thought "we" was the appropriate pronoun. Alex didn't always share the details of cases with me, and in fact, he had one particular case that he had been noticeably silent on. I'd been trying to get used to not asking about it, but keeping my mouth shut still came with great effort.

"I'm going to question the neighbor, Cliff Barber, tomorrow. He's in the hospital overnight, so he must be pretty banged up from his brawl in the backyard with Ben."

"And from your understanding, what was their relationship like? Neighborly?" I stood to fill my cookie container that usually sat full on my table, but had been emptied as we used the snicker-doodles for brain food. Amber and I had made some pecan tarts last week and stuck a few in the freezer. I popped half a dozen of them into my toaster oven and leaned against the counter, waiting for them to soften up on the inside and crisp up on top.

"If they were physically fighting, I don't expect they were on good terms, but Mr. Barber had some trouble talking when the police first pulled the two men apart."

"Wow. And Ben barely had a scratch on him?"

Alex shook his head as he reached down to pet my cat. Hunch wasn't normally very affectionate with anyone except Amber, but when there was an investigation in the works, he pretended to be to listen in on any pertinent information. He had been my late husband's cat and gleaned an interest in solving mysteries—from the ones in Cooper's mystery novels to the real-life versions that Alex solved.

"So you'll wait to talk to Cliff in the morning. Do you mind if I tag along?"

"I was hoping you'd suggest it." Alex's partner rarely rolled out of bed before the crack of noon, so I could usually count on Alex to let me accompany him, at least for the morning investigative work. "I'll pick you up at nine?" He asked it as a question.

I nodded. "And what else is on the agenda?"

"I'd like to do a walk-through of the mansion

DENISE JADEN

first thing, now that forensics has cleared out."

The Honeysuckle Grove forensics team was notorious for missing details, so Alex always made a habit of doing this.

"Plus, I'd like to interview Ben Montrose myself, but since he's in a cell at the moment, I may not be able to bring you along for that one."

I nodded. "Did Detective Bradley make it over to the animal rights association to question them?" When Alex shook his head, I said, "Maybe I could help with that?"

"Why don't you take Amber with you after she's out of school. I have a feeling she'll be itching to get involved with this one, and I'd like to find areas that won't be too upsetting."

He wasn't wrong. Amber had texted me a dozen times since I'd dropped her and her brother's car off at home, begging for information, even though I had little to give her. I hadn't told Alex about my text from Helen Montrose, and I didn't feel like getting into it now. I covered up my discomfort over the subject by chuckling and telling him, "You know her so well."

After we'd filled up on pecan tarts and talked the case to death, so to speak, Alex left and told me I should get some sleep.

I knew I should, and yet I found myself back at my kitchen counter, looking for something to bake.

It was all too much, worrying about whether or not Amber's uncle was somehow involved in a

38

murder and not knowing how much to poke my nose into Alex's investigations. He'd been kind— too kind, in fact—every time I'd asked about the secret case Detective Reinhart had him helping with, but I couldn't seem to stop feeling shirked about it and then asking again. I was always too eager, and I had to wonder when he would put a stop to me helping him at all. He'd gotten in a lot of trouble with his boss already because of me and Amber.

I clearly wasn't ready to take our relationship to the next level, if his reluctance to share details of one single case bothered me so much. And yet, part of me felt as though I wanted to be ready.

That, plus having my fears about Amber's mother finally come to fruition. What if Helen really did forbid her daughter to see me for good? I felt horrible that I'd upended Amber's party. Even if it wasn't what Amber wanted, it had been a show of her mom at least trying.

Plus, I was thinking about the slew of messages my dad had been leaving on my voicemail all weekend. They weren't apologies, either. They were pleas for me to spend Christmas with him. Apparently, my sister, Leslie, informed him that he could only come to her house for Christmas if he convinced me to come. I didn't quite believe that, and yet I didn't have the energy to call Leslie and check. I didn't have the energy for my family at all.

The only thing I had the energy for, I decided as I flipped a page in my recipe book, was some flour, sugar, and a whole lot of butter.

Chapter Five

Morning came too soon, especially because once I convinced myself to go to bed, Hunch kneaded on my stomach, wanting to keep me talking about the case. I'd long ago told him everything I knew, and yet I kept talking well into the night, rehashing it all again and again.

By the time Alex picked me up, I'd made myself some avocado toast and a couple of poached eggs, and baked up a few cheesy scones to bring along for him to enjoy.

I passed one over to him with a napkin when I got into the passenger side of his unmarked police cruiser. The scone was still warm from the oven.

"I can always count on you to keep me well-fed, can't I?" He winked. "Actually, I completely forgot to eat breakfast this morning, so this smells especially amazing."

I grinned. I loved feeding Alex about as much as he loved eating. "You have to remember to eat, Alex."

He took his first bite, and his eyes widened when the cheese melted in his mouth. "So good!" he said with his mouth full. He turned on his windshield wipers to battle the smattering of rain. "I'm glad it's warmed up a little. You never know what the snow was hiding yesterday."

"What about the tiger? Could he have ingested any important evidence?" I'd thought of this question late last night while I'd sat at my table eating sweet and salty pretzel bars and Hunch had finally settled in to eat some kibble.

Alex shrugged as he turned out of town. "I guess that could be said for any amount of evidence. How will we know if the tiger ate anything important on or around Stella? Send forensics back after a day or two and see what he passes? I'm afraid I don't know much about big cats."

I didn't either, even if I'd been learning a lot about a household one. Hunch's nature fascinated me more often than not. "There's a wildlife reserve right off the highway near Harman. Maybe Amber and I could go there and ask a few questions later, too." I kept the fact that Amber may not be helping at all to myself for the moment.

"That would be great." Alex turned down the long road that led to the Montrose mansion. Much of the land in the area was still undeveloped, and there were gaps of space without any houses.

When we arrived at the group of houses surrounding the Montrose mansion, I asked, "Did Mickey speak to all of the neighbors yesterday?"

Alex shook his head. "Most weren't at home, probably Christmas shopping this close to the holidays. Cliff Barber and the lady across the street who called it in, Dorothy Gallagher, were the only people around. I'd like to have another word with her today, and then I'll need to visit Stella's next of kin and find out a little more about her. She had a brother in town. I'm hoping he may have insight into his sister's recent relationship with Ben Montrose."

I hoped not to be along for that part. Coming face to face with newly grieving family members still dredged up my own raw memories.

When Alex pulled into the driveway of Ben Montrose's mansion, the street was much quieter and emptier than it had been the day before, with all the police officers and vehicles gone. In fact, it felt eerily quiet.

"Is that Ben's car?" I pointed to a blue shiny BMW parked at an angle along the right-hand side of the driveway. "Does he usually leave it outside the garage?"

Alex put his unmarked police sedan in park and then pulled a file folder from his console. "Good observation. I'll make a note to ask him that. But yes, that is his vehicle."

"Did it get checked over yesterday?" I wouldn't even know what to look for inside his car. Nail polish remover to wipe away fingerprints? Probably not, but I was still as eager as Alex to find anything the forensics team might have missed.

"It did, but I've got his keys here. We can check again." He passed me a pair of dark blue form-fitting gloves and I put them on, as was habit at any crime scene. Then I stepped out of the car, pulled up the hood on my coat, and followed him toward the BMW. The outside showed nothing significant, and even when Alex opened it up, we couldn't find anything of interest inside. Ben Montrose kept his vehicle pretty spotless.

"Shall we?" Alex motioned to the front door of the mansion.

I led the way up the path, which had been shoveled before yesterday's incident and now barely showed any remnant of snow. "What about Stella's car?" I asked, scanning the neighborhood.

"It's a Toyota, similar to mine, parked down the block."

"Similar to yours? In year?"

Alex nodded. His was a late 90s model.

"Why would she park down the block?" Before Alex could answer, I blurted my next question. "Do you think she was after Ben's money?"

Alex shrugged as he typed a combination of numbers into the keypad beside the mansion's front door. The door clicked open, and a beeping immediately sounded. Alex strode for an interior keypad to punch in a code and stop the alarm.

"Was that panel checked for prints?" I asked.

Alex flipped through his folder and nodded. "No prints on either of the front keypads or the door. The forensics team found a few prints around the house, but they were older and we're pretty sure they will match up with Ben and perhaps Stella from an earlier visit."

"How can you tell they're older?" Forensics science fascinated me.

"They check the degree to which the fatty acids in the fingerprint's ridges have migrated into the valleys. I told them to make it their first priority to find any fresh prints. The only ones they found were those on the backyard gate and a few in the master bedroom."

"Which didn't match up with Ben's or Stella's?"

"They still have to check them against Ben's, but they should be able to do that today."

I went on with my many questions. "Did Ben explicitly say that he'd arrived home *after* Stella was already in the tiger enclosure? The neighbor with the gun said Ben wasn't home, but how did he know that? Could it be the neighbor's prints on the back gate? Also, shouldn't Ben have been the one to want to save his girlfriend?"

Alex skimmed through Mickey's interview reports to answer these questions. "Apparently, Stella had met him at his place a few times, so he'd given her the key and alarm codes. He claims he had not gone into his house yesterday afternoon because he heard noises from the backyard. When he went through the back gate, he saw Stella being attacked and Cliff Barber aiming a handgun at his tiger."

"And he didn't immediately want to save his girlfriend?" I asked again. I looked around the large foyer with a ceiling that reached all the way up to a second floor, trying to picture Stella coming through here yesterday, alone or with someone.

"He said it was clear she was already dead."

My heart stuttered at Alex's words. Alex and Amber both had the ability to think clinically about recent deaths. Me, not so much. "And did he seem upset about it? Or was he only upset for his tiger?"

Alex skimmed his notes again and heaved out a sigh. "You know Mickey. He marks down a half dozen facts and thinks he's done. There's hardly anything here at all about Ben's words or thoughts about Stella Havenshack."

I sighed, too. "Did Ben mention if anyone else knew the entry or alarm codes?"

Alex shook his head. "Mickey didn't ask. Too bad you hadn't been the first detective at the scene. We'd probably have a lot more useful information."

"I don't know about that, but I'm as frustrated as you are by him and your forensics team and their lack of thoroughness."

Alex led the way through the large foyer of the mansion, down a hallway, and into a big, open kitchen. Along the way, I saw little yellow crime scene markers with numbers labeling them. "Forensics is far from incompetent. They're just often dismissed early or sent to other jobs by people like Bradley or Captain Corbett when they assume a case is cut and dried, without studying all the details."

"Two bad apples ruin the whole bunch, huh?"

Alex was doing this thing lately where he tried to keep from rabbit-trailing his derogatory thoughts about his coworkers. More often than not, whenever I criticized them, he changed the subject. "There were water splotches found on the floor from the foyer to the kitchen." Alex pointed to a couple of tented crime scene markers along the floor. "But they also found some on the stairwell and even in the master bedroom."

"So someone wore their wet snowy boots into the house, all the way up the stairs, and into the bedroom? But why?"

"That's what I'm trying to figure out. Ben Montrose said he had not been inside his house yesterday afternoon. He went running straight to the backyard, saw Cliff with the gun, and tackled him to the ground. The police found the two men in a brawl. So that leaves Stella going into the house with her boots on and purposely trekking a fair amount of water throughout the mansion." He looked at his notes. "The water shows up all the way to the sliding glass back door, which was left unlocked, so it makes sense if she came inside, trekked through the house, and then headed out the back entry. The only thing that doesn't add up is the lack of fingerprints."

"If Ben lied about going inside the house first, wouldn't it make sense that the two of them went inside together, got into a fight so suddenly that neither of them had removed their boots, and in the heat of the moment, somehow she ended up in the tiger enclosure? Then he could have wiped all the fingerprints away and made up his story." I took a breath, trying not to imagine the worst. How would Amber handle it if her uncle was actually convicted of his girlfriend's murder? "I'm not saying Ben pushed Stella in there," I said, trying to backtrack. "But if he's lying about coming into the house, it must be to hide something, right?"

Alex nodded. "Of course, we don't have any proof of that. We'll have to question the neighbor who called the police to see if she can confirm exactly when Ben arrived home and which direction he took to the backyard."

"Do we know what kind of terms this neighbor was on with either Ben or Cliff Barber?"

Alex flipped more pages and then made a note. "That's certainly something we should find out."

Alex and I thoroughly searched the mansion, cross-referencing all of the crime scene markers with the notes in his file, not finding anything overlooked.

"I think the forensics team did a thorough job for once," I said as we headed along the upstairs hall to check the master bedroom.

"They were about to leave when I first arrived, at Mickey's direction." Alex let me go ahead into the bedroom, which seemed so neat and tidy I figured Ben Montrose, the bachelor, likely had a maid. "When I told them nothing was cut and dry here, and they were to cover it thoroughly, they ended up staying until almost eleven p.m."

There was only one crime scene marker in the master bedroom, right in the middle of the carpet, but my mind was still on the maid. "Do you know if Ben Montrose employed any help? Perhaps a maid was in here yesterday and left wet marks on the carpet?" When I said it out loud, I realized it would have to be the most incompetent maid in the world to tromp through a house she was responsible for cleaning in wet soppy boots.

"Mickey asked if anyone had been in the house yesterday, but at the time, he understood it was just a matter of Stella wandering into an unlocked tiger enclosure on her own. I can certainly ask more pointed questions about cleaning staff when I interview Ben Montrose." Alex made another note.

"He sure has a lot of antiques." I fingered an old-looking green glass decanter on the chest of drawers with my gloved hand. It was surrounded by five upside-down glasses and a ring of dust where it looked as though a sixth glass had been. We'd seen everything from an antique mahogany rocking chair in the living room to a steering wheel from a Model-T Ford downstairs on the wall. I vaguely recalled Ben Montrose from the one time I'd seen him at Amber's dad's will reading, and he'd been contesting the assignment of some pieces of art. I wondered if they were special or antique. I'd have to check with Amber later.

When we didn't find anything else, we headed back downstairs. Alex made some final notes, set the alarm again, and we left through the rear sliding glass door to check over the backyard once more.

Chapter Six

Today, Boots wasn't hiding. In fact, the full-sized tiger paced right near the fence as we descended the back porch stairs into the backyard. He snarled at us, and I jumped and nearly fell down the bottom three steps. He was bigger than I'd imagined. From nose to tail, he must have been longer than Alex's police cruiser. I wanted to feel pity for such a majestic animal being kept in a too-small enclosure. But all I felt was fear. His name was much too cute for the vicious-looking animal, and yet where his orange-and-black stripes were cut off just above white paws, I could tell how he'd come by his name.

"Why is he out again?" Alex seemed more at ease than me, perhaps because he'd already been acquainted with the large animal yesterday. He shook his head. "I wonder if Mickey told Carson Kroeger he could release him back into the main cage."

"That was the guy from the Department of Agriculture?" When Alex nodded, I asked, "Did something about that guy seem shady to you? I mean, shouldn't someone from the Department of

Agriculture care a little more about a tiger that had mauled someone to death within his jurisdiction? He didn't even consider taking Boots away and putting him somewhere safer."

Alex kept his eyes on the tiger and nodded slowly again. "Maybe you're right. I'll check to see if Mickey's had any interaction with him, or perhaps I should visit his office and have another word with him myself." He sighed. "Regardless, I guess we can't check over anything within the enclosure today."

Truth be told, I wasn't too upset about not having to walk inside that enclosure today. Now that I'd seen the tiger that called it home, just the thought of getting close to the fence gave me chills. "Is this normal in West Virginia? To have a pet tiger?"

My heart rate couldn't seem to calm down, and I couldn't take my eyes away from the large animal. The tiger let out another loud snarl, as though he knew how much he frightened me.

"Not normal, no, but I've come across a half dozen people who have an exotic pet of some kind. I don't get the appeal of owning one myself. Especially if a person can't build an appropriate environment."

I had to agree. And what was the point of keeping a pet you couldn't cuddle or play with?

I laughed inwardly as I thought of my own inherited non-cuddly pet. But at least Hunch wasn't a predator out for my blood.

We kept well clear of the fence. Alex said, "I suppose if we're going to continue to detain Ben Montrose, I'll have to talk to Mr. Kroeger about making arrangements for the caretaking of the animal anyway."

Boots's eyes remained steady on us.

"I think I'll call Animal Control later, too, and see what they know about the Department of Agriculture's regulations."

"Would Animal Control intervene?" I asked.

Alex sighed. "I suppose they could arrange transfer to a zoo that can handle his caretaking. Because he's endangered, I doubt even Animal Control would consider putting him down."

I hated to admit it, but I was glad to hear that. Even if this tiger had killed somebody, I somehow felt in my gut that it hadn't been the tiger's fault, or at least not entirely. As I remembered something Amber told me, I explained it to Alex. "Amber said her uncle used to withhold food from Boots for a couple of days and then throw him a few live chickens in an attempt to keep up his hunting instincts."

"Why would Ben want to keep up his tiger's hunting instincts?" Alex asked.

I looked around the large yard, searching for a reason, but I couldn't come up with one. It was looking more and more likely that Mickey might have been lenient in bringing Ben Montrose in on a charge of gross negligence.

We studied the clumps of lawn that now

peeked out between the snow. We looked in a large deep freezer along the back of the house. It was filled with brown-wrapped packs of meat, all the way to the top.

"Do you think this is the tiger's food?" I asked. Boots banged against the fence, watching us. I forced a deep breath and reminded myself that the enclosure was secure. At least I hoped it was.

Alex nodded and made a note. "Probably."

There was fingerprint dust on the outside. I felt glad that the forensics team seemed to have done a thorough job.

"Was it only Stella's footprints that led to the tiger enclosure gate?" Again, I pictured Ben fighting with Stella and then shoving her into the tiger's cage. Maybe he only wanted to threaten her. I tended to want to think the best of people, which Cooper always said was his main character sleuth's biggest downfall in his mystery novels.

"Only one set, yes, but actually, one outstanding item on my list when I visit Stella's next of kin was to find out her shoe size, as the medical examiner was unable to tell. The boot prints in the snow were pretty large for a woman. Not impossibly large, but—"

"And what size are Ben Montrose's feet?"

Alex looked at me and headed back for the sliding glass door. "Good question. Let's check."

We'd covered the yard and snapped photos of it, now that there was less snow to cover any possible evidence. We agreed that we were done here anyway.

But as we headed toward the back porch again, I had to stop. "Hang on, there's something stuck in my boot."

I leaned against Alex's shoulder as I kicked up my right foot to see the underside of my knee-high black boot. Sure enough, there was a shard of glass stuck into the deep grooves of the sole. I yanked it out and pulled back, surprised. "I think this glass shard is the same color of green as the set of glasses in the master bedroom."

Alex pulled out a paper evidence bag for me to drop it into. "I think you're right." He looked to the upper level of the house. "I'll have forensics come back and take prints from that set of glasses, and I should probably grab one to take in and see if it's a match."

He did that and then we found a dozen pairs of boots and shoes lining a rack in a large front closet. Most were dress shoes, which made sense. Ben worked in law, as his brother, Amber's dad, had, although Ben was more into family law, while his brother had been strictly an injury lawyer.

Alex kneeled and checked the shoes one by one. "All eleven and a half." I didn't know much about men's shoes. Cooper had been a nine, though, and these were all clearly bigger than what I was used to seeing in my front closet. "These are definitely bigger than the footprints we found near the tiger enclosure."

With nothing left to check that we could

think of, I accompanied Alex across the street to question the neighbor who had called the incident into the police.

So far, today's investigative work had added plenty of questions, but not many answers. Perhaps Mrs. Dorothy Gallagher could help.

Chapter Seven

On our way across the street, Alex told me to feel free to ask any questions as they occurred to me. "I'm always happy to have your input, especially if I miss something." We passed an old 80s model Buick in the driveway.

Dorothy Gallagher answered after we had barely knocked, as though she had been watching us and just waiting for us to come to her door.

"What can I do for you, officer?" She had to be nearing seventy, judging by the crow's feet around her eyes when she smiled and her gray hair that was pulled into a bun. She wore an old-fashioned beige dress with orange flowers and a simple tie at the waist. She looked like she was living in another era—maybe the 1910s.

"We have a few more questions about yesterday's incident I'd like to follow up on, Mrs. Gallagher, if you have a few minutes?"

"Of course! Please, call me Dorothy." She swung her door open wide and motioned her arm as though she was offering an array of game show prizes. "And please come in."

"I understand you spoke with my partner, Detective Bradley, yesterday?" Alex introduced himself and then told Dorothy Gallagher I was a special consultant on the case. I tried to quell the blush on my cheeks as I stepped inside and slipped out of my snowy boots. As it had been on my mind, I eyed Dorothy Gallagher's boots near the door. Hers were old-fashioned, but definitely a small woman's size. Then I reminded myself that Dorothy Gallagher had been the one to call the police, probably because she hadn't wanted to go next door and see what was happening herself.

If I'd thought Ben Montrose's house was full of antiques, it was nothing compared to the Gallagher home. Gold-rimmed plates lined her walls, and her entry had two hutches filled with polished silver and wooden items with intricate etchings. At the edge of one of the hutches was a stack of envelopes. The top two were from the electric company and phone company, and both had stamps marked FINAL NOTICE.

She led us to the living room, taking my attention. Her single-arm vintage sofa and mahogany-armed loveseat and armchairs matched the décor perfectly.

"You sure have a large collection of antiques." I motioned to where her souvenir plates continued lining the wall through her living room. "Have you been collecting them long?"

She waved a casual hand. "Oh, yes. My Marvin, God rest his soul, used to take me to shop for a new one down at Chad's each week." She sighed and I sighed inwardly along with her. Losing a husband too soon was unfortunately something I could relate to all too well.

"Chad's?" Alex asked.

"Chad's Antiques on Main. He has a wonderful selection." She sat on the single-arm couch while Alex sat across from her in an armchair. I took the loveseat.

We had gotten off topic, but I suspected Alex was simply being kind by letting her reminisce about her late husband for a moment.

I pulled the pad of paper from my purse and made a note of Chad's Antiques on Main Street. I could drop by and ask about the green glasses we'd found in Ben's house later if Alex didn't have time. I'd snapped a photo of the set with my phone when he went back upstairs to retrieve one to take to the lab.

I thought of a gentle way to bring us around to the subject of importance. "I noticed that Ben from across the street also has a number of antiques. Have you been in his house before to see them?"

She shook her head. "I can't say I make a habit of visiting that man."

Alex glanced at me. "It sounds as though you don't care for Mr. Montrose?"

Dorothy tsked. "Oh, really, I barely know him. He keeps to himself and his possessions."

"How do you feel about him keeping the tiger in his backyard?" Alex asked.

She shook her head. "Why a man can't be

happy with dogs or cats, I'll never know. And now that poor woman was killed."

"Yes." Alex looked down at his notes, as though he couldn't remember Stella's name, but I suspected he was only forming his question. "Are you familiar with Miss Stella Havenshack?"

Dorothy's brow furrowed. "Was that the name of the young thing Ben had been dating?" She looked between me and Alex for further information. "No, I can't say I'd ever met her."

"I understand Ben Montrose was separated from his wife, Roberta. Do you know Mrs. Montrose?" Alex asked.

"Of course, yes. She lived there for years." Dorothy motioned out the large front window across the street and then dropped her voice to almost a whisper. "I can't say I'm surprised she left that husband of hers. I knew he was dating someone else lately, but I didn't know her name."

"You'd seen them come and go together?"

She nodded. "Oh, yes. Seen them, heard them."

"Heard them?" I perked up at the odd phrasing and rejoined the conversation.

"Those two fought like cats and dogs, although I shouldn't have been surprised. Ben and Roberta loved to yell a blue streak at each other, too."

"So loud that you heard them all the way across the street?" Alex made a note in his file.

Dorothy nodded. "Even just last night. I think

59

he had that lady of his inside when Roberta showed up. The Montrose couple made quite a racket, yelling at each other on the front porch."

"Were they arguing about Miss Havenshack?" I asked.

"That's what I thought, but then Roberta kept saying, 'It's my wedding ring!' and 'You'd better give it back!' That's why I'd thought at first it was Roberta sneaking into the place yesterday."

"You saw a woman enter the Montrose home yesterday?" When Dorothy nodded, Alex asked, "Can you tell me if she was alone?"

"Oh, yes, she was."

"What made you think she was sneaking in?" I shifted on the loveseat. While it was likely full of history, it wasn't terribly comfortable.

"Well, for one, she didn't park in the driveway. She also kept looking around as though she didn't want anyone seeing her as she hurried up the front walk and into the house."

"Did she see you?" Alex asked.

Dorothy shook her head. "When I saw her looking around, I tucked behind my drapes to watch. Of course, I couldn't see very much once she'd gone inside."

"Did you keep an eye on the house for any amount of time after that?"

Dorothy shook her head at Alex's question. "No, I went right over to my phone and called Ben Montrose at his office."

I raised my eyebrows. "You called Ben Montrose? But why?"

Dorothy popped out of her chair at my question and moved toward a nearby silver vase on a carved wooden table near the front window. She picked it up, turned it over, and then placed it back down among the other trinkets. "I may not care for the man, but I also didn't think it right of this lady to sneak in while he wasn't there."

"Did you speak to him personally?" Alex asked.

"No. I told his secretary it looked as though someone was sneaking into his house."

"You didn't mention who the intruder was?"

She shook her head. "I figured he'd see for himself soon enough."

I wondered if she'd purposely neglected to give Stella's name to make it seem more urgent. But again, I had to wonder why she was so concerned for a man she didn't seem to care for.

"And you didn't see anyone else come or go before Ben Montrose arrived home yesterday?" Alex confirmed.

"Not a soul."

"Can you go over for me exactly what you saw or heard when Mr. Montrose arrived home, Dorothy?"

She settled into her armchair and looked up at the ceiling. "Well, let me see. It was mid-afternoon, maybe around three, as the sun hadn't yet set. Not ten minutes after I called, his car barreled down the road and into his driveway."

"Did you call out to him or get his attention in any way?" Alex asked.

Dorothy shook her head. "I figured he'd stop by after he confronted her for going into his home unannounced. I figured he'd come over and thank me."

"And so he went in through his front door?" I wondered if Alex was trying to catch Ben in a lie, as he had already told Detective Bradley that he hadn't made it into the house before he heard noises and raced around to the backyard.

"He started to walk for the front door, but then something from the backyard seemed to take his attention." Dorothy's eyes widened with the drama. "He raced around the side of his house, and only a moment later, I heard a gunshot. That's when I called the police."

"Right." Alex nodded and flipped through his file. "And you didn't see anyone else come or go into the house yesterday? You didn't see your neighbor, Cliff Barber, go near the house?"

Dorothy's eyes widened. "No, I didn't even know Mr. Barber was home yesterday."

"Do you know why the Montrose couple split?" I asked. Amber had already filled me in on this part. Roberta had left because Ben loved his possessions, including his tiger, more than he loved his wife. I wondered if Stella felt the same way and she'd intended to hurt the tiger, but it had backfired.

"Couldn't say," Dorothy said. "But he sure was

proud of that big cat. The moment Roberta was out the door, he was asking all the neighbors if they wanted to come by and meet Boots."

"All the neighbors? Including Cliff Barber?"

She scrunched up her nose. "Oh, I don't know that he would have invited him."

"Why not?" Alex watched her intently.

Dorothy shook her head toward the floor and took her time responding. "Cliff Barber loves animals. He used to keep a cage full of rabbits, and a year or two ago, one of his rabbits got out and wandered too close to that tiger cage. The malicious cat took a swipe, and the poor thing bled out before Cliff could get to him. I think he keeps inside cats now."

Amber had told me this story and how Ben had bragged about the fact afterward. No wonder Cliff Barber hadn't wanted to come by to meet the tiger.

"So would you say that Cliff Barber was angry about Ben keeping a tiger?" Alex asked, pressing the point.

"Not more than any of the rest of us, and Mr. Barber wasn't much of an angry man," she explained. "All of the neighbors were resigned. People like Ben Montrose just seem to help themselves to whatever they want in life."

"So Cliff didn't like Ben Montrose?" Alex pressed.

Dorothy shrugged. "I honestly couldn't tell you that, but if I had to guess, I'd say none of the neighborhood had much good to say about him. He is not a very likable man."

"Had Cliff ever used his gun around here before, to your knowledge?" Alex asked.

She furrowed her brow. "Why, no. I can't say I even knew he owned a weapon."

"Did you keep an eye on the Barber house the same way you did with the Montrose one?" I asked.

"I try to keep an eye on the whole street. I'm home all day. I might as well."

"You don't work, Dorothy?" Alex asked.

She tilted her head and shook it. "No, Marvin never wanted me to work."

I wondered if her late husband had left her an insurance settlement to live off after he died, but then I remembered the pile of bills I'd seen near the door. Or perhaps she'd just never been the one in charge of paying the bills and they'd gotten ahead of her. It had been a learning curve for me after Cooper died.

"I'm afraid I can't tell you much else," she said. "Next thing I knew, Detective Bradley was at my door, telling me about the tragedy in Ben's backyard, and they were taking Ben away in handcuffs! Was he somehow responsible for the awful incident with his tiger?"

Alex answered her question with a question. "Would you think Ben capable of instigating something like that?" I'd always admired Alex for his bold questions.

Dorothy looked out the front window again.

When she looked back at Alex, her eyes were resolute. "Yes, detective. Yes, I could."

Alex looked at me with raised eyebrows to see if I had any further questions. I couldn't think of any at the moment, but I had a strong suspicion we would be back.

"Thank you for your help, Mrs. Gallagher. Dorothy," he corrected as he stood. "If we have any further questions, we'll certainly be in touch."

Chapter Eight

We were no sooner back in Alex's car when his partner called and practically demanded that Alex come into the station to debrief. Mickey Bradley had a habit of finding out investigative details from Alex only to take credit for them with his boss, Captain Corbett, who already disliked Alex. I hoped that wouldn't be the case today, but I couldn't argue when Alex told me he should probably at least keep him in the loop and then run his own second interview on Ben Montrose.

When Alex dropped me off at my place, I headed straight for my kitchen table to open my laptop. By the time it booted up and I'd navigated to a Facebook page for the Honeysuckle Grove Animal Rights Association, a fresh pot of coffee was dripping and Hunch sat on the kitchen chair beside me, ears perked up and looking very much like he was reading the screen right along with me.

"These people must be Bruce and Lynda, the couple Amber told me about," I said aloud. They were younger than I expected. Probably not even twenty-five. I scrolled through photos of them and others at demonstrations with signs that read:

SAVE OUR FURRY FRIENDS and END FACTORY FARMING. Even though there were other demonstrators in many of the photos, and even Helen Montrose was in a couple, Bruce and Lynda stood out. They were both blond and athletically lean, but that wasn't it. They had a driven quality on their faces that drew my eyes in every photo.

In one, it was just the two of them standing in the middle of a muddy pen of pigs, and they both had rifles slung over a shoulder. It reminded me of what Amber had told me about how they liked to get their hands dirty.

Next, I navigated to their ABOUT page, where I found their contact info. It included a phone number and email address, but when I saw the location, in the back hallway of the Honeysuckle Grove Library, I made a split-second decision to visit them in person.

I was better at getting a feel for a situation in person, and besides, getting out of the house would distract me from all my wondering about Amber, her mom, Alex, and the case.

"What do you think, Hunch?" I asked as I stood and poured my coffee into a to-go mug. "Want to join me on a trip to the library?"

Hunch never had to be asked twice when there was investigative work to be done. He was scratching at the front door by the time I got there with my purse, coffee, and winter boots pulled on.

"Now, what can we do to disguise you?" Sometimes, when Amber and I took Hunch on a fact-finding mission, Amber brought a duffel bag along for him to tuck into. I didn't have a duffel bag, and I was quite certain wheeling a suitcase into the library would look out of place. I looked in the front closet and found a large orange purse made out of some kind of vinyl. I looked down at my jeans, black boots, and red turtleneck sweater. It wouldn't match and was more of a summer purse, but I was too eager to get going to go change. Hunch was definitely too eager for that. And I figured vinyl was a better choice to visit an animal rights association than any of my leather purses.

It made me feel better as I drove toward the library to have my cat riding shotgun. Hunch truly did have a nose for detective work, not to mention he had saved me from more than one death-defying situation.

I pulled into the library parking lot and watched several young moms walk toward the front entrance with children in tow. "Now you'll have to stay out of sight," I told my cat. I held open my giant orange purse, but he looked down at it as though I was asking him to step into a pit of poisonous snakes. "Come on, Hunch. Otherwise, I'll have to leave you in the car."

He studied me for about two seconds. And then he stepped forward into my bag.

I followed a young mom up the sidewalk toward the library's front entrance. She had two girls who looked like twins in matching pink puffy jackets. I squeezed the top of my purse shut, willing Hunch to stay quiet. If there was one thing that would give Hunch away in an instant, it was preschool girls.

Thankfully, we made it through the front doors and into the library undetected. Right inside, a sandwich board directed parents and kids toward Story Time, off to the right in the children's section. The cacophony that erupted from the story area sounded like anything but a library. Two librarians were busy speaking to moms of particularly rambunctious preschool boys, so I strode by them and toward the rear of the library where there were a few offices.

The rear hallway was much quieter than the front, but I was quickly disappointed to find all of the office doors closed with lights out and no one inside. I navigated on my phone back to the animal rights association's Facebook About page and saw office number 103 listed. I knocked, but 103 was definitely shut tight, without a hint of signage about hours.

I set my purse down, and no surprise, Hunch wriggled his way out of it to sniff around. I didn't mind, as no one seemed to be back here, and perhaps he'd come up with some sort of clue as to how I might locate this Bruce and Lynda.

But Hunch ignored the door to office 103 and instead strode back toward the front area of the library. As he rounded the corner out of the back hallway, I took a dive toward the floor to catch him, but he was too fast. A second later, I was a pancake in the middle of the floor with twenty-some pre-schoolers and their parents silently staring at me with wide eyes.

It only took me a second to realize I was the only spectacle here. Hunch, somehow, had snuck by their keen eyes.

"I...um...tripped," I called, pushing myself up to my knees and then to my feet. My orange purse now hung open along my arm from one strap—not that there was anything left to see inside. "I'm fine. Really." I waved them back toward their business, and thankfully, the librarian took their sudden silence as an opportunity to start reading her first story.

I made my way toward the front desk of the library, checking each row of books along the way for my annoying cat. Finally, I found him down the closest row to the front desk, sticking his nose out as though sniffing around the corner as best as he could without being seen.

I marched toward him, dropped my open purse onto the floor in front of him, and crossed my arms. I swear, his whiskers twitched into a smile as he soft-stepped over the handle of my purse and into its cavern.

After sighing and picking it up, I strode toward the front counter, where one of the librarians was free, now that the children had settled into storytime.

"Excuse me." As I got her attention from where she was checking in books, I felt Hunch wriggling in my bag. I pulled my elbow tight to my side to calm him. "I'm looking for the local animal rights association?"

The lady in a tight salt-and-pepper bun had a name tag that read BARA and looked at me with raised eyebrows. She was slow to answer.

"They're supposed to meet somewhere here?" I motioned toward the back hallway.

"No, they most certainly do not meet here." She huffed, clearly not having much respect for the animal rights couple. Truth be told, I couldn't really envision the wild-eyed, shaggy-haired couple keeping office hours here. "They collect their mail here, I suppose to make them seem legitimate. It's a sneaky way to do business if you ask me."

Hunch wriggled again, and this time, it must have been too obvious for the librarian to miss. Her eyes darted to my handbag, and a scowl deepened onto her face.

"Another one of those rule-breakers, are you?" she asked rhetorically because she didn't leave me time to answer. "There are no animals permitted in our library, ma'am, and I'll ask you to leave and take your pet with you. The people you're looking for are over on Birchwood." She got back to her checking in of books, a dismissal if I'd ever seen one. Before I'd turned to leave, she murmured, "Animals in a library. What are people thinking?"

I sucked in a breath as soon as I was outside. I'd never been a rule-breaker—at least not until I'd started hanging out with Amber. I also wasn't as much in the habit as her of browbeating already irritated people for information. If Amber were here, she'd be back inside, demanding an address for this Bruce and Lynda couple.

Of course, if Amber were here, she'd likely already have a last name and address for them, or easily be able to get that information out of her mother.

I sighed again and headed for my car. What would I do if Amber really wasn't allowed to see me anymore? Would I even be much of a help to Alex on my own, or would he soon tire of my lack of chutzpah? Chances were good that he'd get himself a decent partner eventually and wouldn't need my help anyway.

I set my GPS for Birchwood Street and headed in that direction. No, I wasn't bullheaded or a rule-breaker, but I did at least have a willingness and patience to go knocking door to door if need be. If this Bruce and Lynda couple was keeping an office at the library only as a front, what did that mean? Were they trying to hide something?

I was about to find out.

It turned out, there would be no door-to-door tediousness required. As soon as I turned onto Birchwood Street, I had a pretty good idea of where I was headed. Among the fourplexes and rundown apartment buildings was a single house with a large weathered white fence rimming a yard filled with several animal structures. What looked like a square wooden chicken coop sat at one side of their yard with a wired pen that looked like it could house small goats or pigs on the other. I pulled up along the curb in front of the rundown house. The gate at the front of the fence had a hand-painted sign that read: PLEASE CLOSE GATE BEHIND YOU!!!

This had to be Bruce and Lynda's house. It had to be.

I turned off my car and held open my orange purse, but Hunch had his paws up against the passenger window and growled at me when I told him to get in.

"You know there could be dogs in there, right?"

Hunch wasn't afraid of much, but he loathed the power a dog with any kind of bark and bite held over him. Still, he was not to be held captive in my purse again if he had anything to say about it.

When he still didn't hop in, I said, "Fine. Come along at your own risk because I have no idea what kind of outdoor animals are beyond that fence."

Hunch hopped over to the driver's seat to follow me out on my side. I led the way up to the gate, and my curious cat had already seemingly caught the scent of something because his nose was up in the air, darting in every direction.

"What is it, buddy?" I asked.

Since he couldn't answer me, I continued my trek toward the front door.

Only a second after I knocked, the weathered

front door swung open to the driven blonde, Lynda. She looked from me to Hunch, and then she quickly lost interest in me.

"What are you doing here, sweetie?" She bent to let him smell her fingers.

Hunch purred in response, and I couldn't help the note of jealousy that ran through me, even if he was only putting on a show to get some information. She picked him up, and Hunch purred louder. I looked down at the hand stroking Hunch, lined in short but bright red nails.

"That's my cat, Hunch," I told her, still fixated on her hands. Painted nails, especially of that color, meant owning a good amount of acetone remover.

"Oh. Not a stray?" Before I could answer, she checked his collar.

I wondered how many strays were brought to her door in exactly this way. I didn't have time to think more about that, though, when my earlier question about the outdoor animals was answered by a white chicken clucking around Lynda's ankles. I could see two more in the hallway behind her.

"Are you with the local animal rights association?" I asked.

"Yes. Lynda Oberman." She handed Hunch back to me to deal with moving her chicken back in the house. No sooner had she accomplished that when a goat appeared, nosing his way into the doorway. I wondered how much livestock she had living with her inside her home.

"Mallory Beck," I told her. "You're allowed to have chickens and goats this close to town?" The question fell out of my lips.

"Oh, they're not ours. We rescue animals and sometimes need to care for them for a day or two before locating a humane place for them to go." I was somewhat thankful when she stepped outside onto the porch to speak to me, pulling the door closed behind her, because the waft of barnyard coming from within her house was strong.

"What can I help you with?" she asked. The second Lynda's attention was back on us, Hunch started up his purring once again, even though he was now in my arms. "Are you wanting to join our cause? There's not a lot happening through the winter, other than rescuing the odd animal before they freeze to death, but come spring, we have several protests planned throughout the state."

"You do this throughout West Virginia?" I asked. "I would have thought Honeysuckle Grove was enough of an area to keep an eye on." I said this partly to get her to zone in on local animal rights and partly because I wasn't sure how I should introduce myself quite yet. Should I play the interested activist, or police consultant, or simply a concerned citizen?

"Oh, believe me, it is," she said. "But my husband, Bruce, and I like to run things where we can get a lot of media attention. We find that a protest with a good hook and some exposure causes more lasting change than anything else."

A tiger attack killing a person in town would certainly have accomplished that. But I wasn't sure I could envision this woman going to such extremes as putting someone's life in danger for her cause.

"Lynda," a man called out the front door. I didn't recognize him for the newly grown beard at first, but when he spoke again, I saw the resemblance from the photos on Facebook. "Kroeger's on the phone. What should I tell him?"

"Tell him we're not happy about it, but we'll talk if he's willing to be flexible."

Bruce seemed to notice me as an afterthought. "Oh. Who's this?"

I wondered if "Kroeger" was the same Carson Kroeger I'd met at the Montrose mansion the day before, the one who didn't seem trustworthy. From the way Bruce stood on his front porch, crossed his arms, and narrowed his eyes at me, I wasn't sure I trusted him either.

"Oh, hi!" My voice came out overly peppy. "I'm Mallory. I just met your wife, Lynda, and she was telling me about the great work you do."

That seemed to satisfy Bruce Oberman, and he slipped back into the small house to finish his phone call.

I turned to Lynda. "I have to ask... Are you talking about Carson Kroeger? I just met him yesterday." I raised my eyebrows as though this meeting had been shocking, which, in truth, it had been.

"Oh, don't let him bother you," Lynda said. "You just have to know how to handle him."

Bruce finished with his call, pulled the front door shut behind him, and then descended the two front steps to meet us.

"And how do you handle a man like Carson Kroeger?" I asked Lynda. I kept my eyes purposely from Bruce's, as I could feel his gaze boring into me as though I'd already said or done something wrong.

"Oh, you know the boodle he's after—"

"Who are you, exactly?" Bruce cleared his throat loudly when Lynda started to speak again.

I made a split-second decision to play the police card, in hopes that I could get to the bottom of how the Obermans were connected to the man at the Department of Agriculture. "I'm a special consultant, currently helping the local police with a case—"

Bruce seemed in a habit of interrupting people. At my words, he grabbed Lynda and tugged her toward the house. "We barely know Kroeger. If you're with the police, you should know better than to show up here poking around and asking questions unannounced. Next time you come by, you'll give us a chance to have our lawyers present first, huh?"

With that, he slammed the door in my face.

Which left me to wonder why on earth he thought he needed a lawyer.

Chapter Nine

"Bruce and Lynda know how to handle Carson Kroeger," I said to Hunch on the way back to my place. "What do you suppose that means? Why would they think they needed lawyers present? And what's a 'boodle?' Do you think it's only coincidence that three people we suspect of being involved in a possible murder happen to know one another and two of them clam up as soon as I say I'm with the police?"

I'd thought I'd been investigating some of the periphery information, just to help Alex out, but suddenly, I felt as though I was in the thick of the crucial information.

I called Alex to relay what I'd found out, but he didn't pick up. I sent a quick text, letting him know I had something to tell him about the animal rights angle and to call me when he had a chance.

I felt nervous about doing any more poking around by myself, so I expected to have a couple of hours of downtime to go over my notes and make a plan for when I drove to the high school after three to see if Amber could get permission to come over. Maybe in the meantime I'd do a little cooking.

Cooking always helped clear my head.

But when I slid my key into the lock of my front door, I jumped at a figure that moved from around the hedges and toward me. My heart skipped a beat and then took off at a gallop.

When I saw it was only Amber, I slapped a hand to my chest. "Oh! What are you doing here? You should be in school."

Amber rolled her eyes. "School schmool. The nurse bought my cramps excuse, and no one ever wants to bother my mother, so it really wasn't hard to get the afternoon off. Besides, I don't want to be around when Mom finds out Uncle Ben's been arrested."

The girl snuck around behind her mom's back far more than I was comfortable with.

"If the nurse does decide to bother your mom, though, then what? She already doesn't want you spending time with me."

"Mom has an appointment with her therapist today. She'll definitely drug herself up after and sleep for a good twelve hours." Amber raised a triumphant eyebrow. I suppose she knew her mother better than I did. I still didn't like her sneaking around, but at the same time, I felt out of my depth investigating on my own.

I led the way into the house, changing the subject so I didn't feel so guilty. "Your mom is close to your Uncle Ben?"

"Ha. No." Amber followed me inside as I tried to decide if I should force her to go back to school.

She'd taken one online class this semester to prove to her mom she could handle the workload without a face-to-face class. Her plan was to switch to all online classes in January, if her mom would let her. As far as I was concerned, that hinged on her mom believing she was at least attending her classes this term. "But he's Dad's brother," she went on. "Any reminders of Dad, especially the bad ones, are like a new thing to get over."

That made sense. Hunch sauntered in behind us and licked his front paw, putting on a show like he couldn't care less that Amber was here.

But Amber wasn't one to be fooled, even by the cat that had her wrapped around his little paw. "Hunchie!" She picked him up and snuggled him to her neck, taking a greater risk than I would have with his cranky temperament and razor-sharp claws.

Then again, he was rarely cranky with Amber.

"So what's the plan? I assume we're cooking?"

"Cooking?" I followed her to the kitchen. I figured she'd skipped school to see if she could help with Alex's investigation.

She shrugged and put Hunch down near his food dish. He watched her walk to the sink and wash her hands, uninterested in his food when she was around. "Sure. Whenever we're in the thick of an investigation, you always think it's appropriate to spend a bunch of time cooking up a storm, usually to deliver to a suspect."

She wasn't wrong. I sighed and washed my

hands as well.

"So where'd you go this morning?"

I explained my morning with Alex at her uncle's mansion and questioning the neighbor who had called the police about the gunshot.

"I know who you mean." Amber opened my fridge and scanned the contents, even though she was usually one to let me take the lead on what to cook. "Mrs. Gallagher is always into everyone's business. It used to drive my Aunt Bertie nuts, but Uncle Ben just laughs about her spying."

"Well, for once, her spying might have been helpful. Although I guess it didn't save Stella Havenshack's life, so perhaps not enough so."

I looked over my notes and at the three prospects for us to try and meet with today. I had already done what I could in questioning Bruce and Lynda. As I explained that whole encounter to Amber, I made a quick decision to avoid using the special consultant from the police introduction and focus on my strengths. Who might be swayed by a little baking to get honest with us—the antique store dealer, the head of the wildlife reserve, or Carson Kroeger?

Because I still had the man from the Department of Agriculture on my mind, and it seemed like a real possibility there was something I was missing between him and the animal right rights activists, I wanted to start there.

"What do you think a guy who oversees agriculture would like?" I left my notes on the table and joined Amber in front of the fridge. When I looked back, Hunch hadn't wasted any time in hopping onto my kitchen chair to sniff my note-pad.

"What do we think this Kroeger guy might have to do with it, again?" Amber raised an eye-brow.

"Boots had been let out of his underground lair before we got there today, and Bruce and Lynda both also seemed to know the shady man from the Department of Agriculture."

"Oh. Right." I could tell by her monotone Amber felt like she'd missed a lot in the investigation this morning. In truth, she had, and because I didn't know how to make her feel better about that, I flipped pages in my culinary school cook-book and showed her recipes.

We didn't end up coming up with any culinary ideas for crass Mr. Kroeger, so we focused on what we might also be able to share with the antique shop workers afterward. We decided on salted rum caramel tartlets—for people who ap-preciated the finer things in life. While Amber blended the dry ingredients with butter, brown sugar, egg, and chocolate chips to make the cookie crust, I heated the cream and sugar to thicken a caramel. I think the act of baking was making us both feel better.

Two hours later, I used my kitchen torch for the first time since culinary school to toast the top of the meringue.

"Beautiful!" Amber rarely used such exclamations. The tartlets, which I'd learned to make under the tutelage of an engaging storytelling guest chef from Paris, really were magazine worthy.

"I think these sealable containers will work to deliver them, but each will only fit three." I false-pouted. In truth, after we'd packed up three to-go containers for our afternoon, I didn't mind leaving the other few behind in my own kitchen one bit.

Amber grabbed the containers and rolled her eyes, reading me like a book. "How annoying. That means we'll probably get stuck eating the rest."

"But not now." I shook a finger at her. "We have work to do. These others will be our reward for getting some strong investigative work done today." I guess I wasn't forcing her back to school today after all.

Amber browsed the web as I drove and located the local agricultural department office within one of the municipal buildings. It was right on Main Street, in the town center, and only a short walk from Chad's Antique Village, which I noticed as we passed it.

The Honeysuckle Grove Municipal Office was a two-story standalone brick building, just down from our Town Hall and the mayor's office. We strode into the front lobby, caramel tartlets in hand and without an appointment, and skimmed the directional board by the elevator. The building contained offices for parks and recreation, water and sewage, refuse removal, electricity and gas, and finally, Amber pointed at the words: DEPART-MENT OF AGRICULTURE. It was on the second floor, and Amber and I decided to take the stairs.

"How do we start this conversation?" I asked on our way up.

Amber shrugged. "Let's pretend to be con-cerned for Honeysuckle Grove, with full-grown tigers allowed within the town limits."

"Pretend?" I asked. Tigers were majestic ani-mals, but I didn't like the idea of one being only a few miles from me with only a flimsy wire fence to keep him contained one bit. Especially now that he had a taste for human blood.

"We also need to work Bruce and Lynda Ober-man into the conversation and find out their con-nection." Amber always came up with the best questions. She was too smart for her sixteen years.

Not only that, but she had a way of barreling into a situation that left others wondering what just happened.

When we reached the Agriculture Depart-ment office, she opened the door, strode right up to the receptionist's counter, and said, "We're here to see Mr. Kroeger." Before the receptionist could open her mouth and ask if we had an appoint-ment, Amber held out our container with the lid removed and added, "Salted rum caramel tartlet?"

The lady's face brightened. She reached to take a napkin from Amber and then a tartlet. She had taken her first bite and let out a loud,

"Mmmm," before she remembered that we had asked her for something. "Oh, yes," she said with her mouth full. "I'll check if he can see you."

The lady wore a navy pantsuit, a tidy bob of black hair, and looked like she could probably handle most office responsibilities at any other time, but the caramel delicacy had thrown her off.

She had Mr. Kroeger on the phone and had told him there were a couple of women here to see him before she realized she had no idea who we were or what this was about.

"We're concerned citizens," I told her when she looked up at us blankly.

She passed along the message, and a moment later, she directed us down the hall to an office on the right.

I didn't know for sure if the baking had actually done anything for us until we arrived at Mr. Kroeger's open door and he told us, "I don't usually see people without an appointment." The caramel tartlets had served us well. "Now what can I help you with?"

Amber strode forward with her container outstretched, but the man barely gave it a cursory glance. Then he looked between us with his eyebrows pulled together, waiting for an answer.

I couldn't have imagined anyone dismissing these delicate—and did I mention tasty?—creations so easily, but he didn't even take a second glance at them.

Amber got over the surprise quicker than I

did, replaced the lid, and said, "Yes, my aunt and I are concerned citizens. We heard about a tiger attack out on Clayburn Road."

I thought it risky, her labeling herself as my niece when she actually was Ben Montrose's niece, not to mention the fact that Mr. Kroeger had met me at the crime scene yesterday. But he didn't seem to recognize me. Yesterday, I'd been in Amber's oversized hoodie and leggings with hair that had dried against my head in strange ways. Today, I was much more presentable in my long wool coat and tall boots.

"Well, yes." Mr. Kroeger shuffled papers on his desk as though he was too busy to stop and take a few moments to have a conversation with us. "Let me assure you, that was a one-time freak accident and it won't happen again."

"Is that what the police say?" Amber boldly asked.

Mr. Kroeger ignored Amber's question, turned to me, and pretty much ignored Amber completely, which she wouldn't appreciate. "The tiger in question is fully contained. Our department cannot be held responsible if a citizen opens up and wanders into a tiger enclosure upon their own volition."

I was surprised at his immediate defensiveness. Had someone already suggested that the Department of Agriculture might be held responsible?

"And so that's definitely what happened? A

woman wandered in on her own?" I asked.

Mr. Kroeger blinked up at me a couple of times before answering. "Ma'am, you'll have to speak to the police if you have further questions. All I can tell you is that the tiger's owner had a permit and he kept him in a proper enclosure. That's where our responsibility lies."

"So it had a big enough enclosure?" Amber crossed her arms over her chest. "For a male tiger?"

"I can assure you, miss," he said to Amber, "that all requirements would have been met before issuing a permit—"

She cut him off. "Because we've been talking to Bruce and Lynda at the Honeysuckle Grove Animal Rights Association and I'm not sure they're too happy about the situation."

"The Obermans? Is that what they told you?" His face reddened. "Rest assured, I have spoken with them." At the mention of Bruce and Lynda, he stood and moved toward his office door. "Now, if there's nothing else..."

Amber wasn't deterred. "You're saying Bruce and Lynda are really okay with a male tiger being kept in a too-small cage and then mauling people? And you're okay with that, too?"

It was as though Amber was trying to make up for her absence in the investigation this morning by forcing some answers this afternoon, no matter the fallout. Besides the fact that her questions were clearly agitating this man, I didn't figure she had considered that her words, while they may have shed some responsibility toward the Department of Agriculture, shed a greater deal toward her uncle.

"The Obermans and I have an understanding. They grasp the way governance works, and there are plenty of unpermitted animals for them to spend their efforts on. Let's just let us do our jobs, shall we." As he spoke in his patronizing tone, he actually put his hand on my back to usher us out of his office. "Good day, ladies."

I was about to ask if he'd actually spoken with the Obermans about the incident with the Montrose tiger, but as I turned around, a second door today shut in my face.

Amber was fuming by the time we returned to the parking lot. I suspected most of it had to be due to Mr. Kroeger's tone with her.

"What does that mean, he and the Obermans have an understanding?" I asked as I made some notes before starting up my car.

"It sounds like bribery to me." As soon as Amber said the words, something clicked into place. That was exactly what it sounded like.

"Boodle?" I said it as a question, but saying it out loud made that word click into place as well. "Lynda had said that all Carson Kroeger wanted was 'boodle.' I bet she meant bribe." Amber nodded like I hadn't said anything surprising, so I suspected she was familiar with the term. "But Bruce and Lynda seem so driven to protect animals." I'd already told her about how many they kept in their own house.

Amber shrugged. At least she was calming down some. "I'll bet it's a give-and-take relationship. You said they have a chicken coop and pig pen and live right in town?"

I nodded, understanding dawning on me. "They leave certain people alone, and he, in turn, leaves them alone. But why would Carson Kroeger care to protect your Uncle Ben and his tiger?"

"Well, if he was going to take bribes and deals from anybody, wouldn't it make sense to do that with a dude with plenty of money?"

Chapter Ten

Before we made it down the road to Chad's antique shop, Alex called back, and I filled him in on what we'd found out from the Obermans and Carson Kroeger.

"Good work. I'll get a warrant to check Carson Kroeger's books to see if he's had any payments coming in from either Ben Montrose or Bruce and Lynda Oberman. I'll also have Mickey go over and see if he can get the Obermans to roll over on Kroeger. I think that's something he can handle, and if they're covering up bribes, who knows what else they might be covering up."

I thought again about Lynda Oberman and her bright red nails, the narrow fingerprints on the rear gate of the Montrose yard, and the other doors that had been wiped with a solvent. But before I could express any of those concerns, Alex went on.

"If you're downtown and not busy, get down to the jail." Alex sounded as though he was walking outdoors. "Corbett and Bradley are busy out of the office, so I thought I'd slip in and question Ben Montrose while they're not looking over my shoulder. I'd like to ask a lot of the same questions again to gauge for reactions. I'd love for you to sit in."

"Really?" I looked across the car at Amber, who definitely couldn't be a part of her uncle's follow-up interview. "Oh, but I have Amber with me." She wouldn't be happy about being left out of something else today.

"Bring her along," he said, surprising me. "We'll leave her behind the one-way glass. Maybe she'll notice if her uncle says or does anything suspicious."

I looked for Amber's reaction. This was her family. Did she really want to be responsible for implicating her uncle in someone's death? But she rolled her hand at my gear shift, like *Let's get a move on!*

And so I said goodbye and did exactly that.

Five minutes later, we pulled up to the county jail, which was adjacent to the local police station, right near the downtown core. Alex had mentioned before that the Honeysuckle Grove jail often sat empty, but I wasn't sure that had been the case much since I started getting involved in solving murder investigations.

But was this murder? Or were we blowing things out of proportion? Maybe we'd solved so many murder cases now that I couldn't help seeing situations as anything but. Then again, why wasn't Stella Havenshack's fingerprints anywhere, least of all on the keypad or handle to get into the tiger's cage?

At the very least, there seemed to be more

than first met the eye in this case. This wasn't simply a man with a dangerous pet and a person wandering where they shouldn't.

"What's your Uncle Ben like?" I asked Amber as we got out on either side of my Prius.

She shrugged. "A lot like my dad. Business-driven. A bit of a control freak."

"And what happens when things don't go his way? Your Uncle Ben, I mean. How does he usually react?"

She tipped her head back and forth, thinking this over before answering. "He plays head games with people. That's why I think he didn't have anything to do with this new girlfriend of his getting killed. First of all, Uncle Ben wouldn't have wanted Boots shed in a bad light for anything, and secondly, if he was angry at this Stella lady for any reason, he probably would have just promised to take her to Paris for the weekend, and then once she was all packed and ready to go, he'd pretend he never said such a thing. Something like that to play with her mind."

It made me wonder if Amber's dad had played mind games like that. She seemed to have an example right on the tip of her tongue.

She followed me up the walkway to the jail, and Alex met us at the door. Before we could speak, he motioned Amber along with him, not saying a word himself. He likely didn't want to raise any suspicions about him bringing a teenager into the jailhouse.

The cement block walls made me feel claustrophobic as I followed Alex down a long hallway and into a small room with two chairs facing a large glass window. He was in his plainclothes outfit today, with his suit jacket off and the sleeves of his dress shirt rolled up, like he'd been working hard.

Whenever Alex interviewed suspects or informants at the police station, he either did so in his office or a boardroom down the hall from his office. One look at the interrogation room that sat on the other side of the glass brought back CSI flashbacks. There were recording equipment and laptops on both sides of the glass and a table with two chairs on either side within the clinical interrogation room.

Alex typed something into the laptop near the glass and then turned back to Amber. "You should be able to hear our conversation now." He passed her a set of headphones. "If there's anything you feel like you don't want to hear, just take off the headphones."

Amber rolled her eyes. "What do I do if he says something suspicious? Should I knock on the glass?"

Alex shook his head. "I've got an earpiece in. If you say anything inside this room, I'll hear it." He typed something else into the laptop. "At least now I will. Just try to stay quiet unless it's something that can't wait until later, okay?"

I wanted to offer to wear the earpiece so that

he could concentrate, but I had a feeling Alex was more than competent in handling this part of his job, and I'd be the more likely person to get distracted. He headed for the door.

"You're sure you're okay?" I asked Amber, to which I received another eye roll.

A moment later, I sat down in the chair Alex pointed me to, and he left to retrieve Ben Montrose. I felt odd, having Amber on the other side of the glass where she could see me but I couldn't see her. To lighten the mood, I stood, turned a little pirouette, and then did a curtsy toward the glass. Amber most often wouldn't let on if something was stressful to her, and I couldn't imagine that this interview held no stress at all, even if she was a good actress.

When Alex returned with Ben, it was clear why he'd gotten us situated first. Ben was handcuffed and led by a stern-looking uniformed guard whose name tag read Gerald. Gerald was in his forties and wore a perma-scowl. He didn't look like the type of guard who would have much patience for sneaking a sixteen-year-old girl in to listen in on an interrogation, even if her input might be helpful. I avoided Gerald's eyes as he instructed Ben to sit in the chair catty-corner from me and place his hands on the table.

He obeyed, and his hands remained cuffed when the guard left the room.

"I'll message you when I'm done," Alex told the guard, holding up his phone.

But Gerald, all business, said, "I'll stay right outside. Just give me a knock."

I only hoped he wouldn't decide to kick back and wait in the viewing room. He might not appreciate who he found there.

Alex sat beside me and across the table from Ben Montrose. He tapped into the laptop and, a few seconds later, recited the date and asked Ben to state his full name.

Ben raised his eyebrows in what seemed like a cocky way as he spelled out his last name slowly, even though he hadn't been asked to do so. I recalled what Amber had said about his methods of playing head games.

Alex made a note—since the session was being recorded, I had to guess the note was regarding Ben's attitude—and then asked him to go over everything that had transpired the day before.

"Well, let's see. My alarm went off at six fifteen. I believe I hit snooze. Or was that the day before—"

"Let's start with the phone call you received from Mrs. Dorothy Gallagher," Alex said, unmoved.

He sighed. "My secretary told me a neighbor had called. I assumed it was the nosy Gallagher lady from across the street, trying to stir up excitement. She said she saw an intruder in my house."

"Yet you took it seriously?" Alex asked, surprise evident in his tone.

"Well, sure." He tapped a forefinger on his handcuffs. "If a thief's going to break into a place, which house on Clayburn Road do you think they'd choose?"

"So you figured it was a thief?"

Ben nodded. "Sure. What else could it be?"

Alex pursed his lip, thinking before asking his next question. "Why don't you tell me what you found when you arrived home?"

"Sure. Okay. I pulled into my driveway on the right-hand side. I turned off my car."

I resisted the urge to tap my pen against the table in frustration. But Alex only nodded and said, "Go on." He seemed comfortable with this game-playing suspect.

After a few more nonsense sentences about the temperature in his car and the snow on the ground, he finally got to the part where he got out of his car. "I heard some kind of fuss from my back-yard."

"What kind of fuss?" Alex asked.

"I figured Boots was hungry." Ben shrugged. "But he doesn't usually get so loud and ornery."

"So you heard loud growls?" When Ben nodded, Alex asked, "And so where did you head from your vehicle?"

"Straight to the backyard, of course."

"Through the front door? Is that the fastest path?"

Ben scowled. "No. Through the side gate."

"And what did you see when you arrived in your backyard?"

Ben raised his eyebrows. "I found Cliff Barber

in the middle of my yard, gun poised and ready to shoot at my baby. I didn't think twice. I took the guy down."

I noticed his explanation left noticeably absent the fact that his "baby" had been tearing his girlfriend apart limb from limb at the time.

"Was your intention to injure Mr. Barber?" Alex asked.

"My intent was to get that gun out of his hands. And I accomplished that just fine."

"But it let off a shot in the process?" Alex asked.

Ben shrugged. "I suppose. I was kinda caught up."

"And you weren't concerned with the person being mauled by your pet tiger?" Alex's voice sounded much evener than mine would have. "Did you recognize Stella Havenshack?"

Ben only sighed. "To tell the truth, I didn't notice. I saw the gun, and I saw red. I've had crazy animal activists show up at my place with guns. I wasn't going to let anyone get near Boots with one."

He must have been talking about the Obermans. "When was this? The animal activists with guns?" I blurted.

Ben shrugged. "It started just after I got Boots, years ago, but they've been by lots of times. They'd let up recently, but still, I wasn't going to let anyone else close to him with a weapon."

So the Obermans were clearly familiar with

the Montrose tiger situation. Alex took down more notes. I'd given him a quick overview of my talk with the Obermans, but this was worth discussing again later.

"How long had it been since they'd been by?"

He tapped his finger against the handcuffs again. "I don't know. I suppose it's been a while. Months," he added when it was clear I was going to ask.

As Alex was caught up, I asked another question as it occurred to me. "What time did you arrive home yesterday?" I still had an image of Ben Montrose coming home early, fighting with Stella in the house, and dragging her out to his tiger himself. Then playing dumb about it all and focusing on his altercation with his neighbor.

Ben shrugged. "I don't know. Three-ish?"

"Would you guess before three p.m. or after?" Alex poised a pen above his file. He must have caught on to my thinking.

He shrugged again. I couldn't tell if it was true ignorance or faked. "Oh, let's say six minutes after three."

"And did you immediately recognize your neighbor when you arrived in your backyard?"

"Sure. We all know Cliff Barber—he spends all his time at the gym, but the guy couldn't beat off a flea."

This sounded more like preteen bullying than anything.

Ben went on, and I had to admit, I found his

take on his neighbor very interesting. "He tries to play the bigwig, but I'm pretty sure he's running out of money fast because he's been stealing from my yard."

Now this seemed interesting. "Stealing what?" Alex asked, the same thing I was thinking.

Ben shrugged yet again. I was having a hard time figuring out if that was some kind of tell or if he was just making a concerted effort to look casual. Or perhaps it just ran in the Montrose family —Amber shrugged a lot, after all. I'd have to ask her later. "More than once, I've found meat missing from the freezer I keep for Boots."

"Meat?" Alex and I said at once.

Ben chuckled. "Yup. Cliff's the only person I know who'd steal tiger food. Leave it to a body-builder who's worried about his muscle mass." He laughed as though this was a joke. "But the more concerning part is the antiques I'm missing. They're worth a good chunk of change if you take them to the right dealers."

"So you believe Cliff Barber had been stealing meat from your freezer and antiques from your house to sell because he was broke?" Alex confirmed. "How do you suppose he got inside? Would he have known the key code? Or the code to your alarm?"

Ben shook his head. "Nah, he stole the stuff from outside. My rooster weathervane was one of my favorite pieces."

"Did you keep a lot of antiques outside?" Alex

asked.

Ben rolled his eyes—another Amber-ism. "Sure, sure. The flower planters and water features are nineteenth-century English. My wife, Bertie, picked out most of those and they're hard to move, but I used to have signage, a ladder, and that rooster-head weathervane. They've all gone missing over the last six months, and I don't know who else would have such easy access to my backyard and an interest in frozen meat. I guess I confirmed it yesterday, didn't I?" He chuckled, as if his freedom wasn't on the line.

"So you think Cliff Barber just happened to have wandered into your yard to steal something at the same time that your girlfriend had wandered into the tiger's enclosure?"

Ben's forehead buckled at the question. "I guess I hadn't thought about the coincidence."

"Well, think about it now. Could there have been another reason these occurrences happened at the exact same time?" Alex made a note on his paper, but kept his eyes on Ben—yet another detective skill I was lacking.

"It does seem strange," Ben said slowly. He stared at his cuffed hands where they rested on his lap. The man was difficult to read, probably his lawyerly training, but I could see the instant a revelation hit him. He looked up. "Barber's always been jealous of everything I have. He never liked me having Boots, but I'll bet that was only because he couldn't afford a tiger himself."

I interrupted him. "It wasn't because Boots killed one of his rabbits?"

Ben paused, but he didn't even look at me to answer. He just went on with his own train of thought. "I'll bet he wanted Stella, too. She was a fine-looking lady." His eyes wandered down to the table for a brief pause, but apparently, that was all the remorse he had for his dead girlfriend. He looked up and snapped his fingers, which made the handcuffs clank. "I'll bet Barber followed Stella into my place, tried to hit on her, and when she turned him down, as she certainly would have, he pushed her into the tiger enclosure." Ben's diatribe became impassioned. "Then he tried to shoot Boots to take as much as he could away from me in one fell swoop!"

Alex seemed stunned by Ben's long list of theories for a few seconds, but I was ready to poke holes in them. "Had Mr. Barber ever met your girlfriend prior to this?"

Ben shook his head. "Not to my knowledge. But he must have seen her come and go with me. We'd been dating over a month." He said that as if it were a long time.

When Alex opened his mouth with a new line of questioning, I realized he probably hadn't been stunned with new information. He'd been listening to Amber through his earpiece.

"You said many of the antiques had been chosen by your wife. She didn't want to take them when she left?"

"Ahh, did she ever! That's how I know she'll be back. We just needed a break from each other. She needed to know how much she'd miss me and all the treasures we'd acquired together, that's all."

I squinted. "But you chose to date another woman in the meantime?"

Something didn't add up about his confidence in his marital relationship. Or perhaps he was only playing that up. It was hard to tell with a lawyer.

Ben answered my question, keeping his face directed at Alex as he did. "You know how it is. Sometimes a woman won't know who she wants until she sees someone else has him."

"So you were dating Stella to make your wife jealous?" Alex kept his tone even, although I suspected he didn't care for Ben's suggestions any more than I did.

Ben had no problem agreeing to this statement. "Sure. It was working, too."

"How do you know it was working?" I couldn't help but ask.

Ben smirked, this time at me. "A man knows."

In this short interview, I had a pretty clear picture of Ben Montrose—the man who lived in a mansion among normal-sized homes, who owned a full-grown tiger, no matter the danger to the tiger or others. There was no mystery about why no one in the neighborhood cared for him. Still, just because he was selfish and self-centered, that didn't mean he wasn't telling the truth.

"And had your wife been around your property anytime lately?" Alex asked. "Say in the last week?"

Ben shook his head, but then stopped mid-shake. "Well, sure. Last night, she stopped by. But she didn't come inside. She just wanted her ring back. It was an eighteenth-century piece, in my name, and I made her give it back six months ago when she walked out the door." He looked at me again to say, "I knew that was the part that would really get her crawling back."

It irked me to no end the way Ben Montrose spoke about the women in his life—even the dead one—as though they were his property. But I reminded myself that even if Amber's uncle wasn't the most likable guy, if someone else was responsible for a death in his yard, and especially if it was cold-blooded murder, I planned to bring it to light.

"Who all knows the combination to your home, Mr. Montrose?" There were a few questions Alex and I had talked about asking Ben, and I didn't want to get caught up in his stories and overlook them.

"Stella, Bertie. That's about it."

"About it?" I pressed. "Do you have any cleaning staff?"

He shrugged. "I have a girl that comes once a week, but I don't like to let strangers in when I'm not there. She comes on Wednesday nights when I work from home."

Wednesday was still a couple of days away.

Alex confirmed the full name of his hired

cleaning lady and that she hadn't been by since last Wednesday. Then he got back on the topic of Ben's wife. "So Mrs. Roberta Montrose returned her antique wedding ring six months ago, even though she didn't want to, and then came to ask for it back?"

Ben nodded. "If anyone would've wandered into the tiger cage, it should have been Bertie. I told her Boots would look after the ring for safekeeping until she came back."

My mind whirred, wondering if Stella could have somehow overheard this information and tried to get into the tiger cage without being spotted by Boots herself. "Had Roberta and Stella ever met?" I asked.

This made Ben chuckle. "Sure. Stella used to be Roberta's manager at the shop."

"The shop?" Alex and I asked at once.

"Roberta's flower shop. Obviously, Bertie wasn't going to keep her manager on after I started dating her." He chuckled again. This was all a game to him. In one interview, I had a perfect grasp on what Amber had been telling me about his head games.

"Was the antique ring valuable?" I liked Alex's line of thinking.

"Of course." Ben laughed.

"Do you think Stella could have overheard that you put the ring in the cage with your tiger?"

"Probably. Bertie was yelling a blue streak." This made Ben laugh harder. "Oh, I didn't actually put it in there. I just told her that for fun."

"For...fun?"

Ben looked startled at Alex's tone. "Wait, no. Stella wasn't stupid. Besides, she's not exactly brave when it comes to Boots."

"If the ring wasn't in the tiger enclosure, where was it?" Alex asked.

"Heh. Under an antique glass in my bedroom."

"A glass?" Alex flipped through his file, looking for something.

"How did you know someone wouldn't drink out of the glass and find it?" I asked while he sorted through photos.

"No one drinks out of them. They're radioactive."

I squinted, ready to ask more, but Alex had found the photo of the green glass decanter set from the master bedroom and placed the eight-by-ten in front of Ben.

"Can you tell me anything about this set? It looks antique."

Ben pulled the photo closer toward him, and it was the first time I'd seen him look less than calm and collected. "Where's the missing glass?" He was either surprised or a really good actor.

"We're hoping you can tell us that," Alex said. "Was the set expensive?"

"Not especially." He shook his head, staring at the photo. He tapped his finger against his handcuffs and breathed through his nose. Alex scratched his ear, and it was only after I did a double take at him that I realized he was probably listening to Amber through his earpiece.

"Look, Mr. Montrose." Alex dropped his voice. "This investigation is serious. Right now, we have you on assault and gross negligence, but that may only be the tip of the iceberg. I suggest if you know anything more about this set of glasses, you tell me now."

Ben looked between me and Alex, taking Alex's warning seriously and looking worried. "Why? What does my Vaseline glass have to do with anything?"

Vaseline glass? Seemed like an odd name.

"Do you own any other green glass pieces, Mr. Montrose?"

Ben's scowl deepened. "No. Why?"

Alex pulled another photo out of the file and placed it in front of Ben. This one was a clear photo, probably from within the lab, of the shard of glass that had stuck in my boot. "What I'm concerned about," Alex said smoothly, "is that we found this shard of matching glass in your backyard not far from your tiger enclosure."

Ben stared at the photo for several very long seconds. I didn't think I was imagining his breathing get heavier and more intense.

"Mr. Montrose, what do you know about this glass set and its missing glass?" Alex asked again.

Ben took in one long breath and let it out slowly before answering. "I guess Stella found it. That must be it."

"Found what?" Alex liked to get his suspect to confirm every piece of a puzzle, rather than filling in blanks for them. He was great at that.

"The ring." Ben looked down at his hands. "If the glass is gone, she found it."

I'd thought we were so close, but as soon as he said the words, one big hole in this story left me confused. "If Stella found the ring outside of the tiger enclosure, why wouldn't she have just left with it?"

"Heck if I know." Ben raised his eyebrows at Alex and asked a question so cold, it stunned me. "They didn't find the ring, did they? In her remains?"

"Has Roberta heard what happened to Stella?" I asked, not giving Alex time to answer this.

"Yeah, I told her when I made my one phone call."

He made his one phone call to his wife who had left him? That was curious.

"And what was her reaction? Was she upset?" Alex asked.

"Not especially. Would you be upset if your ex's current romantic interest got torn apart in a tiger's cage?" He said it as though no one would, but Alex and I quieted, as it would most certainly upset both of us.

I wanted to visit Roberta's flower shop, at the very least.

"Who's caring for your tiger in your absence?" I asked.

Ben sighed, as though this was the most up-setting part of the whole conversation. "Bertie said she'd take care of Boots. Reluctantly, of course, but we took a course on tiger care together so she knows what to do."

"I heard you like to withhold food from your tiger regularly. Is that true?"

Ben looked at me and shrugged. "Sure."

His casual response took me off guard, and my next question tumbled out of my mouth in all of its unprofessionalism. "Um. Why?"

Ben sighed as though it was laborious to explain this to me. "It keeps up his hunting instincts." Before I could spit out another flabbergasted *why would you do that,* he explained. "Tigers in captivity are known to get depressed. I had done my due diligence before buying Boots, and I wasn't going to let that happen."

I didn't know if I believed him, but it certainly sounded as though Ben Montrose believed that.

Alex had one more photo to show him. "Do you recognize these pieces of carpet within the tiger enclosure?"

I knew the photo and it wasn't pretty, so I purposely kept my gaze straight on Ben.

His forehead creased. "Sure. That's my new throw rug from the hallway at the bottom of the stairs. Why's it in with Boots?" He seemed genuinely confused by this fact.

"You didn't put it there?" Alex asked. He eyed me in a way that meant he wondered if I had further questions.

I was fairly certain Alex and I would have further questions for Ben Montrose, but for the moment, I offered a nod. I had a slew of things I wanted to ask his niece.

I had gained a lot of respect for Amber in the last half hour—growing up with such sociopathic examples of humans and still turning out so incredibly normal.

Chapter Eleven

The interview took longer than we expected, and we only had a short time to debrief with Amber after our interview before Alex was summoned back to the police station. As we quickly went through Alex's notes, Amber only said, "Yep, that's Uncle Ben," in response to most of the conversation. "I knew he was keeping something from you when he kept tapping his finger, but I'm pretty sure you got everything out of him by the end."

When we got into my Prius on our own, though, I couldn't help but pry a little further into her strange family. "Do you really think your uncle doesn't care at all that his girlfriend was killed?"

"Oh, she wasn't really his *girlfriend*." Amber scrolled through her phone. I didn't know if she was searching up something or just avoiding my gaze.

"What do you mean? Your uncle said she was."

Amber looked up and rolled her eyes. "You heard him. It was all just to get Aunt Bertie back."

"So...Ben and Stella weren't actually an item?"

Amber sighed. "I mean, yeah, they were probably sleeping together. But that was only to sell it to Aunt Bertie."

I squinted. "How are you so balanced in your thinking with so many selfish and driven people in your family?"

She laughed. "Years of therapy." She said it as though she was middle-aged. "When you grow up with narcissistic parents, not to mention an uncle, it didn't take long for my high school counselor to catch on that I needed someone to talk to. You understand. I mean, with your dad and all."

I squinted harder. "My dad?"

She shrugged. "Sure. He's a narcissist. I mean, I've barely met the guy, but when he called the police and ratted you out just because he didn't agree with you, a grown woman, helping with an investigation, then I knew."

"Huh." I sat back into my seat, thinking about that. Even after I'd yelled at my dad and kicked him out of my house, he'd been calling and leaving messages, pretending nothing was wrong in our perfect father/daughter relationship, asking where we should plan to celebrate Christmas. So far I hadn't returned a single one of his calls. I had no idea what to say when he seemed delusional like that.

"Huh," I said again, looking over at Amber. We were already so good for each other in so many ways. It only stood to reason she'd be able to help me understand how to deal with my dad as well.

My phone pinged with a text from Alex.

<**Corbett wants me and Bradley to get over to question Cliff Barber at the hospital. Should we catch up after?**>

I read his text aloud and then wrote him back.

<**Sounds good. Dinner at my place? In the meantime, Amber and I could go look into Roberta's flower shop if you like?**>

A thumbs-up emoji came through quickly, but then nothing else, which likely either meant Alex was in a hurry or his partner was in the room.

"We're good to look into the flower shop," I told Amber, starting up my Prius. "Now we just have to decide if it would be helpful to have you along to question your Aunt Bertie, or should I go in alone as a stranger?"

We decided to go in as the dream team—but as strangers. Often Amber and I posed as aunt and niece when we investigated together, but obviously, that wouldn't work in this case. Instead, we'd decided that Amber would go in first, pretending to be shaken about what was happening with her uncle, and I would come in a few minutes later as a special consultant from the police department.

We'd pretend for a short time not to know each other. Amber assured me that her aunt rarely spoke to her mom or brother, even though they all lived in the same town, so finding out we knew each other wouldn't be an issue. Amber planned to lurk nearby and keep a keen eye on her aunt's body language while I asked a few pointed questions.

Roberta's flower shop was right on the main street of Honeysuckle Grove's downtown core, but I'd never been inside. Even in winter, Roberta had pulled antique wagons filled with winter bouquets outside in front of the glass window. I wondered how the flowers could stand the cold.

I parked down the road, Amber and I went over the most important questions to ask her aunt, and then she hopped out and strode down the sidewalk toward the shop.

I set the timer on my phone for five minutes. If Amber texted me before then, letting me know that the shop was busy and she hadn't had a chance to talk to her aunt yet, then I'd give it a little longer.

But five minutes later, there was no text, so I took a deep breath, went over my questions again from my notepad, and strode for the glass front door.

Along the front window, I saw several arrangements ready to purchase, as well as a sign that read: NO ANIMALS PERMITTED (NOT EVEN SMALL ONES.). It made me pause and think again about how Roberta had apparently left her husband because he cared more about his tiger than he did for her. I wondered if this woman had a grudge against all animals because of it.

A bell jingled as I entered. When I saw Amber and her aunt leaning close toward each other at the till, I had the immediate impression I was interrupting something. But they both looked over at me, so I couldn't back out now.

"May I help you?" Roberta Montrose asked. She was slight, with sleek brown hair halfway down her back, and wore silk pants and a blouse that flowed loosely on her.

"Um, yes." I glanced at Amber for half a second, trying to get a read on if I should stick to the plan. "I just have a few questions."

Amber backed away. "Go ahead," she told her aunt. The shop wasn't much bigger than my kitchen, but Amber moved to the far side, near the front window, and pretended to look over the arrangements.

I met her aunt across the glass counter at the till. "Roberta Montrose?" I asked.

Roberta blinked a few times fast. "Yes." She fidgeted with papers on her glass counter. In only a few seconds, she made up for the lack of anxiety her husband seemed to enjoy.

"I'm a special consultant with the Honeysuckle Grove Police Department. I just have a few questions."

Her eyes narrowed, accentuating her crow's feet, and she leaned in and hissed, "My niece is here!"

Amber wouldn't have been able to hear her low words, but she seemed to have a pretty good sense of her aunt because right then, she called out, "Is it okay if I go in the back and make up a little bouquet for my mom, Aunt Bertie? Flowers always brighten her mood."

"Uh, sure. Yes." She forced a smile at Amber. "Use anything you like."

Amber headed for the back room, not even sparing me a glance. We'd managed to pull the wool over Roberta's eyes about knowing each other, but even with Amber gone, the woman didn't seem at all eager to talk to me.

"I really don't appreciate you interrupting me at work."

I'd learned that if you apologized at the onset of an interview, it could be difficult to regain the upper hand with questioning. "Yes, I understand that, however, we are talking about somebody's life here, and we are trying to get to the bottom of some inconsistencies."

"Inconsistencies?" She went to straighten the papers she'd been gathering, but in doing so, half of them fluttered to the floor. Flustered, she bent to grab them.

"I understand you used to employ Stella Havenshack here at the flower shop?"

She kept her eyes on the papers. "Used to. That's right." Her voice held an edge.

"And how long ago did her employment cease? Was she fired?"

Roberta stood and finally left the papers alone. I wondered, working in a small shop like this one, if she used to be close with Stella. Ben would've really had to be a dirtbag to swoop in and cheat with someone who not only worked for Roberta, but was her confidante as well. "I laid her off a month ago. During the winter, I don't need the extra staff."

I was willing to push for the truth. "Is that the only reason you laid her off?"

Five beats passed, maybe more. I could imagine Amber in the back, throwing flowers together in a bunch, while leaning as close to the doorway as possible to hear her aunt's response. Roberta stared at me, unrelenting, or maybe unbelieving that I would come right out and ask such a question. Finally, she responded. "If you're with the police department, I'm sure you already know my ex-husband had taken up with her."

"Taken up?" Alex had taught me that colloquialisms were the perfect opportunity to repeat someone's words back to them to get them to talk more. I noticed she referred to him as her ex-husband, while Ben had still referred to her as his wife.

"He was sleeping with her, okay?" Roberta moved down the counter away from me, where a cloth lay out with sprigs of greenery atop. She proceeded to pick up each piece and remove the leaves that were imperfect in some way.

I nodded and moved down the counter after her. "And so you let her go from the shop here?"

"Well, I wasn't going to keep paying her, keep pouring out my heartache to her over my estranged husband, now was I?" She grabbed several long-stemmed roses from the counter behind her. In arranging them with the greenery, Roberta poked her finger with a thorn. "Ow!" She sucked on her finger.

But my attention was rapt on something else.

On the back counter, where she'd grabbed the roses, sat a green glass among vases that I was certain matched the set in the Montrose master bedroom.

"That's understandable," I said, my attention divided. "What isn't completely understandable to us…" I always felt out of place when I used the pronoun "us" to talk about myself with the police department, but I didn't retract it. "Is why Ben would have used his one phone call from jail to call his ex-wife, after the woman he'd been sleeping with had just been killed."

Roberta went back for the greenery. The blood from where she'd poked herself was still beading up on her forefinger, but she didn't seem to notice. I noted that her nails were short and unpainted. "Ben and I… we're not typically estranged. We still count on each other."

"And what is he counting on you for now?" I had my notepad out, and I poised my pen above it, ready to write down whatever she told me, even if I suspected it might be a lie.

"He needed me to arrange some money for bail by Wednesday," she said.

"Anything else?" I knew of at least one other chore he'd tasked her with, and couldn't his office have arranged for his bail?

She looked at me blankly for several seconds, but then seemed to clue in. "Oh, yes. And to take care of feeding that stupid cat."

"You mean his tiger, Boots?"

She took in a big breath and let it out in a sigh. "Yes."

"You don't like Boots?" When she shook her head, I asked, "And yet you know how to feed and care for him?"

She nodded. "Ben and I learned about them out at the wildlife reserve before he purchased him. I was always against it. I said a tiger was a dangerous pet, and do you have any idea how much those animals eat?"

Amber had mentioned that part. "A lot?" I said as a guess.

Roberta went on to tell me about the care habits they'd learned for Boots and where they purchased their live chickens in bulk to feed him.

"You fed him live chickens?"

Roberta sighed as though she didn't care to expand. But she did, anyway. "Ben does. We also fed him ground beef, but he eats twenty pounds of meat a day, and Ben was concerned that he keep up his hunting instincts so he wouldn't get depressed."

At least they had the same story in this regard. "And you learned all this from the Harman Wildlife Reserve?" They were on my list to visit as well. When Roberta nodded, I had an extra reason to drive out there. "So you plan to feed him while Ben is detained? Is that a daily job?"

She heaved out another sigh. "As far as I'm

concerned, that stupid cat can stand to miss a meal or two, but I've arranged for him to be fed."

"Arranged? You're not doing it yourself?"

"Believe me, I have no desire to go near that beast. I have a...friend willing to help."

I wondered if that friend was Carson Kroeger from the Department of Agriculture. But for the moment, I had more important questions to press her with. "As far as you're aware, did Stella Havenshack know anything about tiger care?"

Roberta kept her eyes down on her work. It was clear she didn't like talking about Stella. "She was terrified of animals. People used to come in here with small dogs in their arms. I eventually had to post that sign because Stella couldn't hold herself together, even with a little Chihuahua around."

I looked to the curious window sign that indicated pets, even small ones, were not allowed inside the shop. That one tidbit of information told me a couple of things. One, that Stella likely hadn't wandered anywhere near the tiger enclosure of her own free will and this corroborated Ben's claims about that. And two, it was unlikely that she was a part of any type of activist group that protected animals. She definitely wouldn't have wanted to see Boots set free.

It begged the question of why she had dated Ben Montrose at all and gone to his house on her own, knowing he kept a dangerous animal as a pet.

"And so you and Ben are still on amicable

terms?" I confirmed.

She nodded. "You could say that."

"And when was the last time you visited his home?"

She took the greenery and roses back to the other end of the counter, and laid them down on the glass. From there, she started sorting them and pruning them all over again, but this time without the help of any tools. "*Our* home?" She emphasized that it was still hers, and I suppose if they weren't divorced, it partially was. "Well, I sure haven't wanted to be anywhere near there since Stella and Ben got together, I'll tell you that much."

I nodded. "So you haven't been back there in over a month?"

She kept her eyes on her work. "I'd say that's about right."

"You didn't stop by on Saturday night to ask for your ring back?"

She rolled her eyes at me, clearly getting annoyed. "I didn't go inside. Stella's car was in the driveway."

"But you did ask for the ring back?" When she nodded without elaborating, I asked, "And what did Ben tell you?"

Another annoyed eye roll. "That he put it in the cage with Boots for safekeeping." She shook her head. "He was kidding. It was like a cat and mouse game with us. I knew my next move was to ask for the ring back and he'd tease me with it for a week or two before finally breaking up with his floozy and telling me to come and get it. We'd been through this before."

"You'd split up because of another woman before?" I asked, surprised.

She sighed. "I've tried to make a point by leaving. He's tried to make a point by dating someone else. Although, he's never taken up with one of my employees." She murmured the last part.

I hadn't left my spot at the counter and kept eyeing the green glass, wondering how to ask about it. I could sense her frustration with my being here, though, so finally, I just blurted it out. "That's a lovely vase. Where did you get it?"

"This one?" She grabbed a clear vase, not the one I was pointing at. "Oh, these are just from a supplier in the city."

"The green one, too? Is that from a supplier in the city?"

She fumbled with the vases and tucked the green one in behind two other white vases out of sight. "I'm afraid that's one of a kind and it's already spoken for by another customer. But we have plenty of other beautiful vases if you're in the market for an arrangement."

I wasn't sure how much to push. I wanted a closer look at it, but if she refused me and I pushed too hard, she'd likely get rid of it before Alex could come back. "I love flowers," I said. "Not today, but I'll be back." I wondered if my words sounded like a threat. I guess I didn't mind if they did. "All right, well, thank you for answering my questions."

"Good. Are we done, then?"

"For the moment." I headed for the door. "But if there's anything further, either myself or Detective Martinez will be in touch."

I waited in my Prius for nearly half an hour before Amber came out and hopped back into the passenger seat, a gorgeous winter bouquet of amaryllis and Casa Blanca lilies in her hands. "That was crazy," she said. I didn't have time to ask what before she was answering me. "Auntie Bertie is definitely hiding something. And look." Out from under her oversized hoodie, she pulled the green glass she'd somehow smuggled out of the shop.

But she didn't literally have her hands on it, as it was wrapped in tissue. "Do you think we can check Aunt Bertie's fingerprints from this?"

Chapter Twelve

The more important question was if the green glass had come from the Montrose master bedroom, and if it had hidden the antique ring, then where did the green shard out in the backyard come from? The green glass Roberta Montrose had in her flower shop appeared perfectly intact.

We met Alex just down the road from the police department to hand over the possible piece of evidence. It had stopped raining for the moment, so with gloves on, he opened the tissue on the hood of my car and studied the green glass against the eight-by-ten photo from his file.

"It looks like a match," he said. "Now the only problem is getting this into the lab to check for fingerprints and property consistencies without Corbett catching wind of it."

"Why would he care?" Alex's boss, Captain Corbett, was pigheaded and chauvinistic. As if that wasn't enough, he tried to block Alex's path of moving up within the department at every turn. He gave me lots of reasons to dislike him.

Alex sighed. "If he asks how I got it, I'll have to tell him, and you know how he feels about Amber being involved in investigations, not to mention taking the item without permission. I suspect he'll have even more of a problem if he realizes she's family and she's been privy to the details of this investigation."

I tried to come up with an argument for this but couldn't. "So what are you going to do?"

He wrapped the glass up again and placed it in an evidence bag. "I'll log this and submit with the rest, but I won't enter it into the official file quite yet. It doesn't allow me to put a rush on the finger-printing, but one of the lab technicians might just get to it early because it's a quick job. Fingerprints are pretty easy to lift from glass. But the truth is, Roberta Montrose used to live in that house. It's conceivable that they owned a second set of those glasses, or she tracked some down because she liked them so much."

I nodded, hoping that was the case. "I'd love to take a photo of your pictures and go ask about that green glass at the antique store before it closes. Do you mind?"

Alex passed me both of his eight-by-tens, the one of the full decanter set and the one of the shard of glass. "Take these. I can print new ones. Let me know if you find out how common this glass is and if he may have sold some to anyone else in town to his memory."

With that, Alex rushed back toward the fo-rensics lab to covertly submit the new evidence. I wondered if Roberta would notice it missing. She had hidden it behind a couple of white vases, so it was conceivable she wouldn't miss it right away.

Or she may have noticed it as soon as Amber left. Maybe she'd already called her suspicion of me into the police.

Chad's Antique Village wasn't exactly a village, but it was also more than just your average-sized store.

Amber carried the sealable container with our salted rum caramel tartlets, and I led the way under an overhang between two aged buildings into a small courtyard. Growing up in my family, we'd never had a lot of extra money, so antiques had never been my type of shopping spree. I found many old trinkets beautiful, but I just couldn't wrap my head around most of their price tags.

The courtyard was filled with what I had to assume were antique yard structures and tools. Not knowing any better, I would've assumed the shovels leaning against the wall under an over-hang were old and cheap if I'd seen them anywhere else, but I remembered what Ben Montrose said about his outdoor antiques being worth a good chunk of change.

Through the windows of the rooms on either side of us, they appeared to be full to the brim with old trinkets. A carved wooden sign hung over the door straight in front of us that read: WELCOME! FIND CHAD IN HERE. Which left no doubt as to which way we should go.

The door in front of us led to no less of a cluttered space than what we'd seen through the windows. Every single nook and cranny held an old artifact. The whole place didn't appear dusty to the eye, and yet it smelled like it hadn't been swept or dusted in years.

I almost didn't see a man organizing a very full shelf of ornaments until he spoke. "Can I help you find something?"

The thin seventysomething man turned toward us. He had gray hair that fell past his shoulders and thick glasses. His bright smile somehow made him seem much younger than his obvious age.

"We just have a few questions, if you don't mind." I looked around and tried to come up with the correct adjective—one that was honest and yet wouldn't sound derogatory. "It looks like you know your way around antiques."

He chuckled. "Of course! Happy to help. What era are you interested in?" He sounded as though people came in here all the time simply looking for information.

"Actually, I'm not sure." Thankfully, so far I hadn't had to pull the *special consultant from the police department* card to get some answers. "I'm looking for some information on some antique green glassware?" I looked around the store, but it would likely take hours of looking behind and under everything on display to be able to see everything he kept in his "village." I held out the photo of the decanter set to show him.

He snapped his fingers, seemingly knowing exactly what I was talking about. "Vaseline glass. I don't think I have a decanter set, but I have some other pieces in the back."

As soon as he disappeared through a curtain that must have led to one of the other very full rooms, I looked at Amber. Ben had called it by the same name. "Have you ever heard of Vaseline glass?"

Amber shook her head.

Chad returned with a glass candy bowl, much more yellow in color than the pieces I'd seen at Ben's house.

"Oh. No, I was looking for something more green than yellow."

Chad nodded knowingly. "It's all the same stuff. The true name is uranium glass. Most pieces only have about two percent uranium, but some from the twentieth century like this one have up to twenty-five percent." He tried to pass it over to me, but I hesitated, in part because I didn't want him to think I was actually an interested buyer, but in part because the word "uranium" made me not want to touch it.

Ben Montrose had also called it radioactive.

"So these antique ornaments are actually radioactive?" Amber asked exactly what I was thinking.

Chad shrugged with one shoulder. "In a sense. They're probably not going to hurt you, but whenever I sell a piece, I advise not to eat or drink from them. If I had a black light around, it would really freak you out."

When I didn't reach for the bowl, Chad placed it where I would have considered it precarious on the edge of a shelf with several other glass ornaments of a brownish color.

I still had more questions. "Are these uranium glass pieces difficult to come by?"

I figured if Chad only had one in this plethora of antiques, they must be, but he said, "Nah. I used to have a few of them, and I always kept them in the lumber room." I had no idea what a lumber room was, but I was stuck on Chad's confused expression as he scratched his head. "They were so common in the nineteen-thirties a lot of folk still have them as hand-me-downs." He shrugged. "I personally find the color off-putting, but I could swear I used to have more of them."

He wasn't wrong about them being off-putting. I wouldn't want one in my home, especially knowing they even had a hint of radioactivity. Who would put flowers into a vase like that? But then I remembered Roberta Montrose may have been lying about her intention to use the glass for that purpose.

"Amber's uncle, Ben Montrose, he has a set of Vaseline glass pieces," I said, watching for recognition.

"Ah, yes, Ben and Bertie? They used to shop here all the time before, well, you know..." He dropped to a whisper. "Before they split up."

Amber and I both nodded solemnly. I tried to wait out an appropriate length pause before asking, "Did he buy this decanter set here?"

Chad raised his eyebrows and then slid behind a glass counter so littered with antiques, I didn't see the laptop until he started typing into it. "Let's see now." He pulled his glasses down his nose to see better. Several seconds later, he shook his head. "Afraid not from me, no."

"And has Roberta Montrose ever been in to purchase anything on her own?"

He looked over his screen again and shook his head.

"Are you the only antique dealer in town?" Amber asked.

Chad puffed out his small chest. "Sure am."

"And you're sure he didn't purchase it here?"

He looked over his screen one more time at my question, but then shook his head. "They travel a lot. The glassware's not uncommon, so they could have gotten it from any antique shop, really."

"Any other locals you know that have purchased Vaseline glass from your store?" I motioned to his laptop.

He had a long look over his screen. "Not for at least a year. I'm implementing a new inventory system because I seem to have things go missing so often these days."

At the thought of antiques going missing, I blurted my next question as soon as it occurred to me. "Do you know a man named Cliff Barber? Has he ever shopped here or sold any antiques to you?"

"I don't know the name..." He scrolled through a few screens on his laptop and finally confirmed the fact. "Nope. I can't say I've worked with a Mr. Barber."

Amber thumbed over her phone and a few seconds later, turned a Facebook page toward him. I got a quick glance at the name, Cliff Barber, and the muscular guy in the photo.

Chad shook his head. "Doesn't look familiar, I'm afraid. Is he a local antique aficionado? I'm sure I'm familiar with most of them."

"I thought he could be," I said. "But then you must know Dorothy Gallagher and her late husband...?" I snapped, searching for his name, but Chad filled in the blank.

"Of course! Marvin and Dot used to be some of my biggest customers." Chad looked down and shook his head, taking a moment to mourn his customer's passing. "Dot still comes in here from time to time. She likes it when I tell her stories about where the different pieces came from and find ones that she can see the intricate differences between. Old folk like us, we like to prove our eyesight and brains aren't failing, even if our bodies sometimes are." He let out a light chuckle.

"But you've never sold her any Vaseline glass?" I wasn't sure why I was asking this. It wasn't as though Dorothy Gallagher had reason or the ability to throw a much younger and stronger Stella Havenshack into a tiger enclosure.

Chad shook his head. "It would have shown up on my inventory list if I had. She hasn't bought a piece since Marvin passed, but I don't mind the company from someone who enjoys the old artifacts as much as I do."

"Thank you for your help," Amber said, making it clear we'd likely learned all we could from Chad. She passed over the sealable container. "My Aunt Mallory's a chef, and she made you a little treat for answering our questions." Sometimes Amber liked to get all the credit for our baking. Not today, apparently.

We made our way to the door as he thanked Amber and peeked inside. "What are they?"

I could smell their aroma all the way across the small shop and to the door. It made me want to rush home and help myself to one or two of ours.

While I was lost in thought, Amber answered. "Little drops of heaven. Trust me."

Chapter Thirteen

On our drive out of town, I made Amber go over my notes and every word of my conversation with her aunt to try and pinpoint more accurately what she might have been hiding and why, but Amber said there were so many things that seemed wrong that she couldn't put her finger on it.

"From the first moment I walked in, it seemed like she didn't want me there. Especially when I told her I heard something about Uncle Ben and wanted to come to the source."

"Did she have to be prodded to tell you he was in jail?" I guessed.

"No, that part she admitted right away. It was the part about why that seemed to make her tongue-tied. Maybe she didn't want me to imagine the gory details. After all, she had no idea I'd been right at the crime scene and had a good look at the carnage left behind."

As hard as Alex and I had worked to keep Amber away from seeing the mess inside the tiger enclosure, she had been too quick and nimble for us to keep track of at the crime scene.

"But you don't think that was it?" I guessed by her unconvinced tone.

She shook her head. "I don't know. I mean, she liked Boots at first. At least, when I'd been over to meet him, she'd been just as proud of that cat as Uncle Ben, but today she acted like she'd only ever gotten him for Uncle Ben. And she had to be pretty angry with Uncle Ben and Stella for hooking up. I suppose it makes sense, her trying to change the subject." Amber twisted her lips, still trying to pinpoint all the things that were off about the interview.

"Do you think that glass was from the set in the master bedroom? And if so, when do you think she took it?" So far I had avoided coming right out and asking if Amber thought her aunt capable of murdering Stella Havenshack. But these questions could certainly lead in that direction. Then again, Amber was the one who had taken the glass to check her aunt's fingerprints.

She nodded. "The lab will be able to prove for sure if it's a match. If it is, she would've had to have gotten it sometime between Saturday night and when the police showed up Sunday to investigate Stella's death, right? If Alex goes back in to put pressure on Aunt Bertie, she'll tell the truth. I'm pretty sure about that."

I hoped Amber was right. I also hoped her aunt hadn't killed her uncle's girlfriend in a fit of anger or passion, but my hope in that area had started to dwindle. "What do you think about her explanation of why Ben called her first from the station?"

Amber nodded. "I can buy that. With his girl of the month out of the picture, he needed someone to follow his orders."

"Orders? Is that how you'd describe their relationship?"

She shrugged. "I don't know. It's complicated. They loved each other. Still do, I'm pretty sure. Rather than coming right out and saying it, they play these games. Aunt Bertie walks out on him to try and prove a point, and then Uncle Ben starts dating her employee to prove his own point. All the while, it's just a game to see who can't live without who the most. I guess that turned out to be Uncle Ben when he got stuck in the slammer." Amber tilted her head as though this was a surprising revelation. "Then again, Uncle Ben was always the type of guy who couldn't be alone. Aunt Bertie should've known that."

I mentally went through my conversation with Roberta. "So her anger at Stella was certainly justified." Which meant she had motive, I thought but didn't say. "I'm not so sure about her forgiving Ben so quickly, but if you say it's normal..." I changed lanes. "What did you think about Stella's fear of animals? Did you buy that?"

Amber shrugged. "Hard to tell. I never met Stella, but couldn't Alex find that out from her next of kin?"

I nodded. "Good idea. Do you want to text him

with an update and ask him?"

She picked up her phone and typed. "Are we headed to the wildlife reserve now? Should I tell him that?"

"Yeah. I suppose we could probably get just as much information about tiger care from the Internet, but now that I've heard Ben and Roberta took a training course out there, it gives me an extra reason to want to go ask some questions in person."

"We could also ask them if they know Bruce and Lynda Oberman. You'd think the local animal activists would have something to say about the reserve. I wonder if they've ever shown up out there with guns."

"I wonder," I agreed.

As I drove, she told me about the last time she'd been out to the wildlife reserve, when she was eleven and went on a class trip. I'd never been, so I listened as she explained how they were located outside of town so the biggest animals had lots of area to roam.

"But they didn't actually have tigers?" I confirmed.

She shook her head. "No exotic animals. They took us on a guided tour, and they had big murals of lions and tigers and cougars. One kid asked when we'd see the real lions. The tour guide told us big predators were too hard and expensive to care for. We got stuck looking at porcupines, bald eagles, and wild pigs all day."

I found it curious that the people running the reserve would have a tiger training course if they didn't actually care for any tigers. But we were only ten minutes away by that point, so I figured I might as well ask about this in person.

Chapter Fourteen

Amber wasn't kidding about the wildlife reserve being on a large plot of land. The driveway off the main road wound around for at least two miles before we found the entrance. Thankfully, it hadn't snowed since yesterday, and the long driveway had been cleared at some point. Amber had called on the way to see if anyone was here, as they wouldn't be open for tours until the spring.

The man on the phone assured Amber that there was always someone on the premises, but if we were coming in the next hour, he'd meet us at the reserve office to talk to us himself.

The office looked more like a small shack than an actual office. I parked in front of it, and a second later, a very good-looking man with a rugged beard and a red plaid jacket moved through the door and out onto a weathered porch to greet us. He reminded me of Hugh Jackman.

"Hi!" I called as I got out of the car and immediately flushed from my exuberant tone.

"Mallory Beck?" Along with his good looks, he had an outback Australian accent. Oh, dear. That was going to make it even harder to keep the flush off my face.

"Yes, that's me. And this is my niece, Amber." Thankfully, bringing Amber into this conversation had the face-cooling effect I was looking for. But one glance at her told me she was equally smitten.

He held out a hand. "Stan Roseland. How can I be of service today?"

Again, I was stunned by his musical voice, and when several seconds passed and I didn't say anything, Amber stepped in. "Have you ever met a couple named Bruce and Lynda Oberman?"

"The Obermans? Sure, yeah, yeah. They're out here all the time." From Stan's jovial tone, I had a hard time thinking the Obermans had ever shown up on his property carrying weapons.

"You're on good terms with them?" I guessed.

"Sure. In fact, they were just out here yesterday. We've got a couple of groundhogs coming in February and I wanted to get their opinion on the habitat."

"Yesterday? What time?" Amber said the words before I could. If the Obermans were here yesterday afternoon, they couldn't have been on Ben Montrose's property.

Stan pursed his lips, thinking. "Around one?"

That would have still given them time to get back to the Montrose property by three.

But then Stan added, "They helped me dig some holes for the little guys to burrow into. Not so easy digging holes in the middle of December, but they assured me it was only going to get colder and the ground harder. The groundhogs would appreciate it."

"So how long were they here?" Amber asked.

Stan tilted his head. "We were done by dark. Four thirty or five?" he guessed.

"And they were with you the entire time?" That was long enough after three that it had to at least clear the Obermans of being at the Montrose property themselves.

"Sure. Well, not right here, but a few miles into the reserve. We took the tractor, as the terrain out there can be rough."

I changed topics. "We have a few questions about tiger care, but I understand you don't keep any exotic animals here at the reserve."

Stan took in a breath and let it out in a sigh. "We're not a zoo, Ms. Beck. I'm afraid we don't *keep* animals, at least not in the way you're thinking." The distaste in his tone was evident.

I felt bad for how I'd phrased it, but only a second later, indignation took over. "Well, I'm sorry for my poor phrasing, but why would you hold instructional courses on caring for tigers if you don't have any experience in caring for them yourself?"

His forehead creased. "Instructional courses?"

My heart skipped a beat. Had Ben Montrose lied about his tiger training course? If so, what did that mean?

"Are you saying that you never took a Mr. Ben Montrose through a training course on how to care for a pet tiger?"

DENISE JADEN

He pulled back. "I have never..." But then he trailed off, looking off into the distance for a long moment thinking. He pursed his lips again. "Montrose. That name sounds familiar."

I was glad I hadn't introduced Amber with her last name. If I needed to, I'd add the "special consultant to the police" designation to mine.

"Ben and Roberta Montrose. They claimed to have taken a course here prior to purchasing their pet tiger," I added to urge him to search his brain—or any paperwork inside his office.

Stan's eyes widened with sudden recognition. "That was no course, I'm afraid!"

It was cold outside. I hoped Stan would invite us into his small shack of an office. I hoped it was heated. But as we waited for more, he only stood shaking his head.

"If it wasn't a course, what was it?" Amber pushed.

Stan sighed again. "This Ben Montrose you're talking about—I remember him. He made an appointment a few years back to come out and meet with me. Didn't tell me much of what it was about, only that he had some questions about local tigers and wanted to know how educated I was on the subject. I told him back in Queensland I used to help with a program that bred tigers for conservation. The guy drove out here, wanting to pick my brain, or so I thought. But when he arrived with his wife, it seemed more like he turned every bit of information I gave him around to convince his wife that he should *buy* himself a tiger. The guy must be some kind of salesman because he talked circles around both me and his wife."

"He's a lawyer," I told Stan, if only to make him feel better. "So it wasn't your intention to help him figure out care for his pet tiger?"

"Absolutely not. The man lived in a community. I told him that even a female tiger needed a good five acres. A male tiger would be unpredictable and lose his mental stability if kept in a smaller space than several square miles. The guy laughed at that suggestion. I remember as much. Then I tried to convince him against it by telling him how much meat a tiger would consume every day. He turned that around by reminding his wife of the chicken plant near their acreage." Stan shook his head. "I tried to convince them out of it. Believe me, I tried."

"Ben mentioned withholding food for a few days and then feeding his tiger live chickens to keep up his hunting instincts. Is that something you would have recommended?" I asked.

Stan sighed loudly. "I certainly didn't suggest withholding food, no. But I probably would have told him that if tigers aren't allowed to roam and hunt for their food, they'd get depressed. It's a common problem with big cats kept in captivity."

I had to admit, I was surprised that Ben had been truthful on this point, even if the way he'd chosen to keep and care for his tiger hadn't been optimal.

"But in the end, his wife was behind him acquiring a pet tiger?" Amber asked.

Stan looked up, searching his memory. "I don't think she was exactly in favor of it. But it seemed like she was getting tired of arguing the guy. To be honest, I was, too. The worst part was, when he first arrived, I had no idea he was considering a *pet* for himself, and so I actually gave him examples of the horrors I've seen of people breeding them without proper safety measures or space, bribing agriculture departments to get permits, and all just to make a buck. Chances are good that I helped him actually find the cat he was looking for."

"Wow, I'm really sorry to hear that," I said. "Thank you for your candidness, and believe me, this is not your fault." I wanted to make sure to get this through to Stan. Soon enough, he'd hear the news that a woman was mauled to death by a pet tiger in Honeysuckle Grove and I wouldn't want him to feel responsible. "You're right. Ben Montrose can talk circles around almost anybody."

Chapter Fifteen

On the drive back to Honeysuckle Grove, I was angry. Amber seemed resigned.

"Yeah, my Dad's family, they all kind of see the world in whatever way suits them." Now that she put it like that, it definitely resonated with my own dad.

"How do you deal with people like that?" I honestly wanted to know. Even though we had an investigation to solve, seeing these traits so starkly in Amber's family made me need to know more, both for Amber and for myself.

She shrugged. "Don't take on their baggage. They're going to live their lives the way they want to anyway, so you just check out of their decision-making in any way you can. Cut your emotional ties."

I thought back to my last argument with my dad, trying to understand what this would look like.

Amber must have grasped my difficulty in understanding because she went on to explain. "Whenever my dad said he felt like I wasn't around the house enough, I told him he was entitled to his feelings, rather than arguing him or validating what he said. My therapist taught me that."

"Do you still see your therapist?" It sounded like she had some great ideas that I could use.

"Nah. I mean, she's there if I need her, but now I just make an appointment if I'm stressing out about something. I haven't seen her since a couple months after my dad died. I'll get you her number, though."

"Thanks." I was about to ask more when Amber changed the subject.

"So that wildlife guy had it going on, huh?" She picked at her nails, so I couldn't tell if she was just telling me *she* thought he was hot or if she was asking me. She always had a roundabout way of trying to get to my feelings about Alex, and I suspected this was another case like that. I wished I could answer her honestly, but I still had complicated feelings that even I didn't understand where Alex was concerned.

"Stan? Yeah, he reminded me of Hugh Jackman," I said.

She scrunched her nose, obviously disagreeing.

"Not that it matters. He lives way out here and seems pretty singly focused on his job."

"That could change. If he met the right woman."

Now she was really confusing me. Was she trying to sway me away from Alex? Maybe she was concerned that if Alex and I started dating, she would get left in the dust. But it was impossible to dispel this idea, no matter how wrong it might be, without having the conversation outright. So I said, "For now, I'm pretty happy with my Three Amigos relationship."

I winked at her, but she only murmured, "For now," and then looked out the passenger window.

By the time we drove back into the municipal limits of Honeysuckle Grove, we had gotten talking again and discussed everything Stan had told us about the Obermans and his conversation with Ben and Roberta Montrose.

"I think we can safely clear the Obermans of suspicion if they were way out at the wildlife reserve."

Amber said, "But then why were they so jumpy when you told them you were with the police?"

"It had been right after I asked about Carson Kroeger. I'm not saying they haven't been doing anything wrong. I'll bet when Alex gets a look at Mr. Kroeger's books, he'll see they were all doing plenty wrong. I just don't think they could have been the ones interfering with Stella or the tiger enclosure yesterday."

Amber's feeling was that her uncle and aunt simply saw the world through their only lens, and from their point of view, they hadn't actually lied to us or the police about it being a "course" they had taken from Stan. She added, "But if one of them is actually responsible for that woman's death, then they should definitely pay," so I knew she wasn't so connected that she couldn't have a clear head about it.

As I turned down the block toward my house, she changed the subject. "What are we making Detective Martinez for dinner?" If she were a few years older, she most certainly would be crushing hard on Detective Alex Martinez. Sometimes I thought she was anyway.

"My fridge is stocked." I kept it that way regularly. Whenever Amber wasn't too busy with homework, she spent the evenings at my house having cooking lessons. Not that she really needed lessons anymore, but we both appreciated the company. "What do you suggest?"

She twisted her lips, thinking. "Something to combat the cold? Stew?"

I nodded as I pulled into my driveway. "Stew often tastes better slow-cooked to let the flavors really sink into the meat. But I like the way you're thinking. What about a goulash, with some fresh baked bread?"

"Mmm." Amber was out of my passenger door and headed for the house when I'd barely gotten my car into park.

Hunch waited on his haunches, just inside my foyer. If anything could make Amber forget about good food, it was my cat. In two big strides, she had him up and cuddled into her arms. It had taken some convincing—with both of them—for him to stay home for the afternoon, but I was glad I stuck to my guns because Hunch would have spent hours waiting for us in the cold car.

"I'm sorry we couldn't come back and get you today, Hunchie. Tomorrow you can come and investigate with us, okay?"

Hunch nuzzled her neck and purred, but I had no doubt he was taking in every word of that promise. We hadn't even decided where we would be going tomorrow—*after* school, because I had to insist on that much—but apparently, now it would have to be a cat-friendly location.

She headed for the kitchen. "Do you already have ground beef thawed?"

I'd bought some fresh yesterday. My boots took longer to pull off, so I called, "In the fridge."

By the time I got to the kitchen, Amber had onions, garlic, and the ground beef on the counter, and she paged through my culinary school recipe book, looking for goulash.

I shook my head. "I use my grandma's recipe." I pulled a small recipe box from the window sill and handed her a card. My grandmother on my dad's side was about the best family I had—besides my sister, Leslie. I often marveled that the kind, generous woman had raised such a self-centered son. "But we should start on the bread first, so it has time to rise."

Amber nodded and set the oven to warm. Then she headed for the pantry for the bread flour. We'd baked fresh bread half a dozen times, so Amber could likely do it without a recipe, but I'd long ago stressed the importance of exact measurements for baking, so she reached for my culinary school book a second time and flipped right to the dog-eared page.

"I'm just going to go clean up, okay?"

She nodded. I didn't need to shower or change, particularly, but it always gave Amber an extra nudge of confidence when I left her alone in the kitchen to get her bearings and not feel like I was always looking over her shoulder to direct her.

By the time I returned to the kitchen, Amber had kneaded the dough and it was rising in the warm oven because my kitchen was too cold. She had garlic and onions simmering on the stove.

"I'll make a fresh tomato sauce for it." I ignored the cans of tomato sauce she'd retrieved from the pantry and instead grabbed for the bag of Romas in my fruit bowl.

She watched me as I boiled some water, cut an X on the bottom of my tomatoes, and then tossed them in for a minute. When they went into the ice bath next, their skins came off easily. Amber was great at splitting her attention between her own cooking and keeping a keen eye on whatever I was doing. She would make a great chef if she decided not to go into detective work when she was done with school.

I got my own chopped onion frying as she sautéed the ground beef. I added some finely chopped garlic and carrot to sweeten the sauce and to lower the acidity. Once I'd added and cooked the

MURDER AT THE MONTROSE MANSION

tomatoes and herbs into the sauce, it was ready to go into my food processor and then add to the goulash. By this time, Amber had a couple of cups of macaroni noodles boiling in another pot.

"Mmm, it smells *so* good," she said.

It did. Hunch sat on one of my kitchen chairs, watching our procedures, as though that might give him some hint of what we had been up to today.

"Don't worry, Hunch," I told him. "Alex will be here soon and we'll talk through all the details of the case."

But by the time we had the goulash compiled and warming on the stove, and the bread baking in the oven, I had a new text from Alex.

<Not sure I'm going to make it over. I have to meet someone at my place. Should we talk by phone later?>

I read the text aloud to Amber as I surveyed the kitchen. She was busy scrubbing pots and the kitchen was almost clean, but she stopped and turned toward me, her face downcast. "Seriously?"

I hated to see Amber disappointed, so I reached for a solution. "Why don't I text and see if we can bring dinner by his place later?" In truth, not only was I eager to see Alex in person, but I'd never seen where he lived. I always tried to picture him when he went home and couldn't. But I wanted to.

<Let me know when you're done with your appointment. If you want, Amber and I could

bring dinner by. I mean, you have to eat, right?>

I hoped it sounded casual and fun, and not too pushy. A second later, I received a reply.

<You just made my day. I hated having to cancel on yours and Amber's cooking. How about seven o'clock at my place?>

He followed it up with an address. It had a number twenty-two in front of it, so I wondered if it was an apartment or a townhouse. I wasn't sure why, but I'd always pictured him in his own freestanding house—not something easy for most West Virginians to afford on a single salary, I realized now.

I relayed the information, and Amber immediately beamed. "Can we bring Hunch?"

I laughed. "Since this is our first invitation to Detective Martinez's place, I think we'd better leave our pets at home."

For all I knew, Alex wasn't allowed pets. Or maybe he had his own.

Chapter Sixteen

An hour later, we packed up my Prius with all the piping hot food wrapped in towels in the backseat. The goulash's flavor was a little more developed because of the extra time—not that anyone without a super picky palette would notice.

We'd spent the last hour talking through the details of the case, mostly for Hunch's benefit, so he'd let us leave without a fight. But it was also good for us to rehash the information and make sure we hadn't missed anything.

"If Stella Havenshack was really afraid of all animals, isn't it pretty likely that someone would have had to force her into the tiger enclosure?" Amber had asked this question a few times in different ways over the last hour. I was having trouble proclaiming this investigation a murder and letting Amber's brain run wild with that before we'd gone over all the details with Alex.

"If your aunt was being truthful about that," I said as I followed my GPS's directions toward Alex's place. "Let's remember, your aunt had motivation to lie to try and make the woman who was dating her husband look bad, and as far as she's concerned, I was not an actual police officer."

In truth, I still saw Roberta Montrose as the most likely suspect. She had motive. We could tell by her having the green glass that she'd had opportunity. The only thing I wasn't completely certain about was the means. Roberta was a slight woman. Could she have forced Stella into the tiger enclosure against her will?

Amber nodded and thought this over. I turned the corner to a row of picturesque two-tone brown townhouses, each with a tiny plot of lawn out front. I immediately could envision Alex walking up one of the front walkways at the end of a long day.

I pulled up along the curb when number twenty-two came into view across the street. I figured Alex must park his Toyota in the back because I didn't see it. I turned to Amber, about to suggest she grab the bread loaf and salad, while I took the goulash in the slow cooker, but when I did, she looked past me and her mouth dropped open. "Who's that?"

I followed her gaze to where Alex now stood on his front porch, talking to a shapely, blonde woman. Whatever she was saying to him, he shook his head in response. He hadn't noticed us sitting in my car across the road. Then again, it was hard to notice anything past the striking blonde. She wore thigh-high black patten boots that didn't look warm enough for the weather, along with a tight royal blue sweater dress that showed off her curves. Her coat was slung over her arm, even though she must have been turning into an icicle.

I swallowed. "I guess that's the person he had to meet. Maybe it's for a case." Even as I said the words, I knew they were probably only wishful thinking.

"We should get in there before the food gets cold." Before I could argue about trying to stay invisible for another minute, Amber jumped out of the car, reached into the backseat, and pulled out the bread and salad. Just like a teenager to barrel through an uncomfortable situation without thinking twice. I didn't have as much confidence and preferred to take my discomfort in bite-size pieces.

Amber strode across the street, calling, "Hi, Detective Martinez!" before I was even out of the car. A second later, she moved past him and the blonde, and through his open front door.

Shoot. If I'd been smart, I would have hurried along with her and let her absorb the better part of the discomfort. Now both Alex and the blonde stared across the street at me.

To hide my flush, I bent into the backseat to grab the slow cooker. When I turned back around, the blonde had re-angled so she was blocking my view of Alex. Or his of me.

Alex repeatedly glanced over her shoulder toward me, regardless. I figured the faster I moved past them, the least distraction I would be, so I hurried across the street, up the path to his townhouse, and then stood at the bottom of the four steps that led up to the porch.

"I'm really sorry if we're early," I said, even though I was quite sure we were right on time. "I won't interrupt. I'll just go plug this in so it stays warm."

Alex stepped away from the blonde to allow me room to pass between them. "No problem. We're almost done. Mallory, this is Taryn. Taryn, Mallory."

He motioned between us, but the blonde wore a tight smile and didn't say a word when I said, "Hello, nice to meet you," to her. This was not a business meeting. I was quite certain of that. Had Alex double-booked himself with a date tonight?

But I shook off my inner questions, nodded to both of them, and took my slow cooker through the door. I had to place the cooker on the floor in his entry to pull off my boots. When I did, the blonde—Taryn—reached for the knob and pulled the door shut between us.

Before it closed, she said, "I'll let you get back to your food delivery lady, but I want you to think about what I said, Alex. Morgantown has opportunities for both of us."

My face hit three hundred degrees. She'd pegged me as a food delivery person and spelled that out to Alex? The worst part was that she was probably justified. I'd been cooking for the last two hours and had my hair still pulled back with a headband. I wore jeans with frays around the pockets and a plain gray sweatshirt. I *looked* like the hired help, especially next to that well-put-together woman.

Amber returned from what must have been the kitchen to find me still pulling off my second boot. She reached for the slow cooker. "Did you find out who that was?" she asked toward the door with a sneer.

I feared her voice might carry, so the second my boot was off, I led her back toward the kitchen. "No idea, but I'm sure Alex will tell us about her when he's done."

On the way to the kitchen, I got a glimpse of Alex's living room. A rumpled blanket lay on the couch, and I could picture him there, watching the news or a late-night talk show, decompressing after a long day at work. Otherwise, it was tidy. A small dining room sat beside that, with a spotless table. The room looked as though it was rarely used. Through an open doorway, we arrived in the kitchen.

The kitchen felt more bachelor-esque than the rest of the house. A few dirty coffee cups littered the counter, and the small kitchen table was covered in papers. I could envision Alex rushing through here first thing in the morning, taking sips of coffee as he prepared for the day and then rushed out the door.

Amber set the slow cooker on the counter and plugged it in. "Low?" she asked.

"Just set it on Keep Warm. We don't want the noodles getting mushy."

She did as instructed and then tossed the tin-foiled loaf of bread between her hands. "Where do you suppose Alex keeps his cutting board?"

I felt uncomfortable going into his stuff, even if it was only his kitchen. "Why don't you set the salad on the dining room table for now. We can ask him when he's done."

She rolled her eyes at me and started pulling open cupboards and drawers. Eventually, she found a cutting board under the sink and a bread knife in a drawer. I was at a standstill for far too long, but her casualness soon rubbed off on me. I took a breath, moved forward, and searched cupboards for bowls and side plates.

By the time Alex returned inside, Amber and I had set the table, dressed the salad so it was ready to serve, and sliced the bread.

"Something smells amazing!" he said. "Although I shouldn't be surprised, should I?" When he laughed, there was a bit of discomfort in it.

"It's just goulash and bread," I said, waving a hand. Amber was usually the one to make these false modesty statements, but I wasn't myself since walking in here. "Nice place you have."

Alex barely seemed to notice my compliment. Instead, he strode straight for the kitchen table, gathered the papers atop into a big messy pile, and then turned to face me, blocking the pile with his body, as if I suddenly wouldn't know the mess was there.

Didn't he know I saw his mess of papers as a sign of his dedication to his work? I certainly didn't see him as messy. The rest of his house was pretty spotless.

"It's okay," I said and motioned with my chin, referring to the pile behind him.

But this only made him turn and gather up the papers in his arms. One of the ones on top had a header that read: DEEDS OFFICE. I recalled how I'd found a title deed under my late husband's name that I hadn't known about. I'd mentioned it to Alex, but I never had looked into it.

I was about to ask if he was familiar with the local deeds office and if he could get me in touch with them when he said, "I should really put these upstairs. I'll be right back." With that, he disappeared out of the kitchen and up a stairway in a flash.

Whether he was uncomfortable by being interrupted with the blonde or having left a mess on his table for us to see, I wasn't sure, but I brought the ceramic pot from the slow cooker to the dining room table where Amber was arranging cutlery. My mind remained on Alex's strange display. Did those papers have something to do with the blonde woman? Something he didn't want me to see? Maybe he was seriously considering selling his place and moving to Morgantown.

I swallowed and took a seat. There was nothing left to do but wait for Alex. He didn't take long, anyway, and he seemed more relaxed when he joined us at the table.

"Goulash, you say?" He took a seat across from me and beside Amber. He sniffed in a deep breath and let it out in a happy sigh. "Thank you, ladies, so much for bringing this over. I'm starving."

Those words seemed to make everything feel a little more casual, and we passed around and divvied up food. Alex spooned three heaping spoonfuls into his mouth before he spoke again.

"This is delicious!" His mouth was still full.

"My grandma's recipe," I told him when I finished chewing a bite of bread.

He pointed with his spoon. "I like your grandma."

He probably wouldn't like her so much if he knew she was responsible for raising my dad. After all, my dad had caused some pretty major problems for Alex at the police department the last time he was in town.

"So...why don't you tell me what you were both up to today, and then I'll tell you about my strange interviews with Cliff Barber's doctor and Stella Havenshack's brother."

I still wanted to ask about the blonde at his door, but I supposed we had more important things to focus on. Amber began by filling Alex in on our trip to the antique shop, the uranium glass we learned about, our meeting with her aunt, and finally, everything Stan had told us at the wildlife reserve.

"When we interviewed Ben, he really made it sound as though it was a scheduled program. But it's good to hear he can account for the Obermans. I'll get Mickey to follow up on that tomorrow. He's been looking into Carson Kroeger."

If Alex had passed Mr. Kroeger off on his partner, it must mean he no longer viewed him as guilty of more than just taking bribes.

"I got out to Rick Havenshack's place earlier this afternoon," Alex said. "He was pretty broken up about his sister, but at the same time, I got the distinct impression he wasn't all that surprised."

"No?" I asked.

"He works as a landscaper. Told me that both he and his sister loved plants and so he thought working at a flower shop would be a good fit for her, but now he wishes she'd never gotten involved with the Montrose family." Alex looked at Amber. "Sorry."

Amber shrugged, like this really didn't bother her. "So he wasn't surprised she got killed because he always expected problems with my aunt and uncle? Does that make sense?" Amber was great at separating herself from situations, even when they were super personal, but I was especially proud of her now for asking this question, like she was fully willing to admit if she wasn't seeing the situation clearly.

"Rick said he never trusted Ben or Roberta. Roberta kept promising Stella raises and never gave them. Then Ben started dating her and actually paid for her rent and groceries because he said she shouldn't suffer because of his wife's jealousy. He promised to take her on vacations and even told her he planned to give her Roberta's antique ring."

"The ring?" Amber and I said at once.

Alex nodded. "So she was definitely familiar with the ring, and her brother was constantly telling her not to trust Ben, so my theory is that when she heard how badly Roberta wanted the ring back, she snuck into his house to find it and take it, in case he changed his mind."

It was a good theory. And what if Roberta showed up at the exact same time to get the ring, they fought over it, and then Stella ended up in the tiger enclosure? I decided not to say this out loud quite yet, but if I got Alex alone, I would tell him my theory.

"What about Stella's fear of animals?" Amber asked. "Did you get my text about that?"

Alex nodded. "Rick confirmed that she's always been terrified of animals. Apparently, their parents kept a watchdog when they were young that snapped at anything that moved, including a preschool-age Stella. She hasn't liked them ever since."

"And her parents?" I asked. "Where are they?"

"In Ohio somewhere. Apparently, they are very self-serving people. They pretty much abandoned their kids when Rick turned eighteen, and he made enough money back then mowing lawns and doing yardwork to support both himself and his sister, who was still in high school at the time. Stella had never been much of a go-getter, and he said he wasn't surprised at all to see her falling for Ben and Roberta's empty promises. She'd always been looking for someone to take care of her the way her parents never did."

I shook my head as Stella Havenshack became a fully formed person to me. We all had our difficulties to face in life, but it sounded as though she'd had more than her fair share. And Ben and Roberta Montrose had exploited that.

As we continued to go over the details, the food disappeared quickly. Amber slipped into the kitchen to retrieve the banana cream pie we'd made for dessert.

Alex rubbed his stomach. "At this rate, I'm going to have to roll into work tomorrow."

Over dessert, Alex went on to tell us about his interview with Cliff Barber's doctor. "They have Cliff in the psychiatric ward, and it took me a good part of the day to speak to the doctor in charge of his case."

"Psychiatric ward? There was no room for him in emergency?" I'd read news articles about the Honeysuckle Grove Hospital being too small for the size of the county it was responsible for, and how patients were often treated in hallways or wherever they could fit them.

But Alex shook his head. "No, Mickey's report made it sound as though he'd been brought in for physical injury, but apparently, once he had been checked over in emergency with only a couple of bruised ribs, he checked himself into the psychiatric ward. I expect this was due to trauma. He did watch a woman get mauled to death by a tiger, after all. But I got the impression from the familiarity of the nurses that this was not his first time in the ward."

"Could his doctor confirm that?" I asked.

Alex shook his head again. "Confidentiality laws prevented him from telling me pretty much anything. However, as I left the hospital, I overheard two nurses talking about someone named 'Barber' and using the words 'muscle dysmorphia.'"

I looked to Amber, but she didn't seem any more familiar with the term than I did.

We both looked back to Alex, and he went on. "I Googled it when I got back to the station. It's a condition not unlike anorexia nervosa."

I squinted. "He's a skinny guy? I thought he was a bodybuilder?" The guy Amber had found on Facebook to show Chad at the antique shop had been heavily muscled, anyway. But now I started to doubt we'd had the right guy.

Alex nodded. "He is a bodybuilder. It's like anorexia in that it's a misperception of the body. If this was indeed Cliff Barber they were talking about, and if he indeed has this condition, it's likely that he doesn't see himself as strong or powerful, even with the amount of muscle he has."

"That lines up with the way Ben talked about

him, as though it hadn't been hard to tackle and overtake him," I said.

"And with him stealing meat from my uncle's freezer. If he didn't feel muscular enough, maybe he was desperate to eat more protein and couldn't afford to eat a lot any other way," Amber added.

Alex nodded. "His doctor assured me he would contact me whenever Cliff is up to speaking to me. He hinted that might be as soon as tomorrow."

I shook my head. "I don't know, the fact that Cliff is so difficult to get access to, it raises red flags for me. What if he threw Stella into the tiger enclosure and now he's avoiding the police the only way he knows how, by checking himself into the psych ward?"

"It's certainly a possibility," Alex allowed. "But as far as I understand things, Cliff had never met Stella Havenshack. I can't imagine he would kill the woman, and in such a violent way without a strong motive."

I finished a bite of pie before saying, "That makes sense."

"Can you get a warrant to search his house?" Amber asked.

Alex shook his head. "Not without probable cause. Plus, what would we be looking for?"

"A freezer full of meat? Stolen antiques?" I put my fork down. I wouldn't be eating anymore with so many interesting details on the table.

"It's interesting that Dorothy Gallagher's the

one who really likes antiques," Amber said. "I wonder if Cliff could have been stealing them from Uncle Ben and selling them to her?"

"If that's even a possibility, we could go back and grill Dorothy Gallagher. Maybe we could find out from her if Cliff would have had any possible motive to kill Stella Havenshack." I was never usually so forward with my suggestions, but I felt like we were close, which made me eager.

Amber was noticeably quiet through this whole conversation. She had school tomorrow. It was her last week before Christmas break, but still, that sort of thing never kept her from begging to be right in the thick of an investigation.

But as she finished her pie, all she said as she cleared her plate was, "Let me know what you find out from that Gallagher woman."

Chapter Seventeen

On the drive home, I had to ask what was going through Amber's big orchestrated brain. Because there had to be more to her simple compliance. However, straightforward questions rarely got anything more than a sarcastic response out of her.

"Busy week at school before the Christmas break?"

She looked out the passenger window. "Not especially. I have a couple of essays due, but I'm already done with them."

This didn't surprise me. Despite the amount of time she spent at my house cooking or helping with investigations, she had a good grasp on time management and seemed to be sailing through high school with close to straight A's.

"That's good." I drove for a few more minutes, but couldn't come up with another nonchalant question. Besides, Amber could most often see right through me.

Finally, I just came out with it. "I'm surprised you didn't say you wanted to come to the Gallagher house tomorrow, too. I figured maybe you were finally getting your priorities in check." I winked, so she knew I was joking. The girl, after losing her dad in the summer and keeping her upheaved family life running smoothly since then, did better with keeping her priorities straight than anyone I knew.

She smirked. "Oh, I'm coming. Sorry, did you miss that?"

I looked away from the road to raise an eyebrow at her. We were at a red light, so I didn't relent for several long seconds. "What do you mean?"

She shrugged, but I had to look away to drive. "I knew it would be weird for three of us to go in there for a second interview, and you know what to look for as much as I do with the antiques."

"Okay, so...?" She liked to create extra drama by leaving her sentences hanging. At the same time, it worked very well when we questioned suspects or informants, so I didn't exactly want her to change.

"So I'll just need you to tell Alex you'll drive me to school and then meet him at Gallagher house in the morning."

"So you are going to school?" She wasn't making sense.

She scowled. "I'm going to the Gallagher place. After that, I'll go to school if I have to." I started to interrupt, but she wouldn't let me. "Don't worry, I'll duck. Detective Martinez won't even know I'm there."

"But, Amber, he's in charge of this investiga-

MURDER AT THE MONTROSE MANSION

tion. Don't you think we should be upfront with him about our plans? Besides, if you don't plan on coming inside to interview Dorothy Gallagher, what exactly will you be doing?"

I pulled up to her house. Without discussing it, I'd driven here because I didn't want to get in any more hot water with her mother than I was already in.

"I'll tell you in the morning." She sighed. "Better to ask forgiveness than permission, in my experience." It's what she often said about her mother, and I had to agree that, in that instance, she was often right. Her mom wasn't always thinking clearly these days, and Amber had a good head on her shoulders. Plus, she had me.

But I really didn't like keeping things from Alex. By her next words, I realized neither did she.

"Look, Uncle Ben said his stolen antiques were outdoor pieces, right? I'm just going to snoop around Cliff Barber's and Dorothy Gallagher's backyards while you're both inside. We'll bring Hunch, see what he can sniff out." I hated to admit it, but her suggestion to bring my cat did somehow put my mind at ease, at least a little. "We'll stay out of sight. If Mr. Barber's not home and if Mrs. Gallagher happens to spot me, I'll say I was over to see my Uncle Ben but he wasn't home. I'll claim to know nothing about where he is or what's happened in the last couple of days and I'll say that Hunch went running off into her yard, so I was simply trying to grab him."

Wow, she'd come up with all of that while silently cleaning up pie plates at Alex's? I had to admit, it did sound like the perfect excuse. As though she didn't know if she'd convinced me, she went on.

"Detective Martinez could get in a lot of trouble for involving a teenager. I know that. So I'm just doing this on my own. It's my uncle and I want to help in any way I can, but I'm not about to get Alex in trouble for it. Plus, how much trouble would he have to go through to get a warrant to search their backyards? This'll save him the time and the trouble. Don't worry. I'll tell him right after, especially if I find anything."

I did worry. But at the same time, Amber was right. If we wanted to get to the bottom of whether or not Cliff Barber was hiding out in the psychiatric ward to avoid the police, this might be the smartest way to do it.

Chapter Eighteen

When Amber got into my car early the next morning, she spoke to Hunch before she even said good morning to me.

"Now, you're on special assignment today, Hunchie. We'll go over the details again, but you need to have your sniffer in its top shape to find anything suspicious." She had Hunch up on his hind legs on her lap so she could look him in the eye.

"My sniffer's in top shape, and I smell something bacon-y and amazing," I told her.

"Oh. Yeah." She passed me a casserole dish covered in foil. "Bacon and cheddar breakfast muffins. Help yourself."

I loved the glow of pride on her face when she'd chosen and cooked something all on her own. "Mmm!" I helped myself to one. "Where's this recipe from? Is it mine?"

She shook her head. "I saw it last week on a cooking show. I did my best to remember it because they didn't post it on their website."

Not only had she gotten up to cook early this morning, but she'd also been investigating websites to do it. Two big bites and the bacon-y good-ness was gone. I'd definitely have another, but I decided to get us there before I changed my mind about her coming along.

We drove across town and to the outskirts to-ward Clayburn Road, where Ben Montrose's man-sion was located. It had rained again overnight, which hopefully cleared more of the snow to make it easier for Amber to find any outdoor evidence. I could tell at her neckline that she'd layered at least three hoodies under her down coat. The one on top was black, and the large yellow letters read: BAD DECISIONS MAKE GREAT STORIES.

I hoped that wouldn't be true for today.

"Now you're going to stay out of sight, right?" I tended to babble when I was nervous, especially when Amber was trespassing, which was more often than I cared to think about.

"Yes, *Mom.*" She picked up Hunch, who had been lying on her lap for the car ride, and looked him in the eyes again. "We'll be super covert, won't we, Hunchie?"

There was a pause, like we were both waiting for my cat to answer. Honestly, it wouldn't have surprised me much.

I pulled over a quarter of a mile before the Montrose mansion. "I don't think I should let you out any closer if you want to go in undetected. Your uncle mentioned how observant and into everyone's business Dorothy Gallagher is."

She shrugged. "We don't mind walking, do

we, Hunch?" Again with the extended pause. Then she reached for the door handle.

"Should we meet back here? Or how will I find you?" I asked.

She looked at me like I didn't have my brain turned on. "Text me when you're done."

Right. There was such a thing as technology. A teenager would never let you forget that.

Seconds later, she placed Hunch down on the ground, about to shut the car door, but Hunch widened his eyes up at her.

"Oh, yeah. I guess I should have mentioned. Winter is not Hunch's favorite season." Being outside town, there was still some snow lining either side of the road. He picked up his front paws one by one and looked at them as if willing the cold white stuff to just get off him.

Amber laughed and picked him up. "Well, I guess it's a good thing *I* don't mind walking then. But you'd better get over it quick, Hunchie, because I need some help investigating."

She strode away with Hunch in her arms, and my nervousness about Dorothy Gallagher spotting her was quickly overshadowed by one of the other neighbors calling the police about a trespasser when she ducked between two nearby houses.

I held out my phone, wondering if I should text her and warn her to only trespass in the Gallagher yard, but then rethought it. Amber was smart. Even if she did get caught, she had the ability to don a cherub-like innocence that allowed her to get away with almost anything.

I took in a breath and put my car back in drive to edge along until I reached the Montrose mansion, and then a dozen feet past it, where the Gallagher house sat across the street. I didn't know if this would be a surprise visit or if Alex was planning on calling ahead, and I'd purposely arrived ten minutes early to let Amber out before Alex arrived, so instead of pulling into the Gallagher driveway, I drove past it and pulled up to a curb, just beyond the next house.

I checked my phone again, but there was nothing. I tried to breathe easier and remind myself that no news was good news. No news meant Alex still planned to meet me here. It also meant Amber had likely stayed out of sight of any of the neighbors.

As I looked around, there weren't many vehicles in driveways, so there was a good chance most of the neighborhood had already left for work.

Finally, in my rearview mirror, I saw Alex pull up in his unmarked sedan and turn into the Gallagher driveway.

So not a surprise visit, at least not anymore. I slipped my phone into my purse, double-checked for my notepad and pen, and then hopped out, so he'd know I was already here.

Before leaving my car behind, I remembered Amber's breakfast muffins and grabbed them from the back. It turned out, they wouldn't be warm by the time he ate them because when I arrived at his car and handed them over, saying, "Here. Breakfast," his mind was clearly on the investigation at hand. He simply nodded his thanks and put them on the passenger seat for later.

In truth, I was glad not to have to expound on them. I wanted to give Amber the credit, and yet, if I said she'd baked them this morning, that might lead to a whole slew of questions about dropping her off at school. I hated lying to Alex.

"Listen, when we go in there, follow my lead, okay?" he said.

I nodded. "Does Dorothy know we're coming?" I asked. But a second later, I didn't need to because Dorothy Gallagher stood on her front porch, waving to us.

"Detective Martinez, Mrs. Beck. Do come in." Her voice sounded sweet and helpful.

She swung open her door, and Alex and I hurried up the porch steps and inside.

"Now you said on the phone there had been some new developments? And you think somehow I can help with those?" She hadn't even given us time to get out of our boots.

Alex led the way toward the living room. My boots always took a little extra time to get out of, but in this case, I was stalling to investigate the foyer's antiques a little closer. "I'll be right behind you." I waved them both ahead to the living room.

"Well, before we get started..." Alex's voice carried from the living room. "I should tell you, Ms.

Gallagher, that we believe foul play has played a part in Miss Havenshack's death."

"Foul play?" Shock leaked out in her voice. "What are you saying, detective?"

I gave a once-over to the foyer's antiques and snapped some quick photos with my phone. There was a decanter with four glasses surrounding it, similar but not identical to the set we'd found in Ben Montrose's master bedroom, but this set was made of pink glass and had silver etching along the sides. There was also a blue vase filled with dried hydrangeas. Beside the vase was a fancily engraved wooden plaque with two empty hooks on the front that looked like they should hold something. I looked all around the hutch it was sitting on and the floor around it, but it didn't seem anything had fallen off. None of these could be outdoor antiques from the Montrose yard.

"I believe we're upgrading the case to murder," Alex said from the other room.

Dorothy Gallagher gasped, and then her questions tumbled out, one after another. "What on earth? What do you mean? Why would someone want to murder that woman, and why in Ben's yard?" She gasped again. "You don't think he did it?"

As Alex tried to calm her down with niceties that didn't give her any answers, I figured if Amber could poke around a little bit, maybe I could too. I crept toward a closed door down the hallway, just to peek inside.

As soon as I had the door cracked open an inch, a waft of some kind of cleaner hit my nose. The room was filled with bookcases, and each shelf held so many silver teapots or ceramic figurines or glassware sets that they were crammed full. There were enough old trinkets here, she could open her own antique shop. Not only that, but outdoor antiques such as shovels and ornate garden chairs sat in the middle of the small room. I even noted a couple of bowls made of that Vaseline glass.

And on a table right inside the door sat an unmarked silver can with a screw top. I reached for it to see if that held the same strong-smelling cleaner, but the second I did, Dorothy's curt voice sounded from behind me.

"Mrs. Beck? Is everything okay?"

I snatched my hand back and pulled the door closed. "Oh, I was just going to slip into your bathroom quickly first, if you don't mind?"

She studied me for a long moment before saying, "There's one right off of my kitchen. Here, let me show you."

She led the way back down the hallway from where I had come. There was another doorway, but it was shut, and I got a glimpse of her old-fashioned red and white kitchen, but a second later, she showed me the tiny bathroom.

"Thank you," I told her and slipped inside.

The bathroom held more antiques—an ancient-looking plunger, several silver bells, but also a couple of Vaseline glass woman-shaped figurines on a shelf behind the toilet. I looked up from there and saw a weathervane with a rooster on it that was attached to the wall. Ben Montrose had told us about a rooster weathervane—a favorite piece of his. I pulled out my phone and snapped a couple of photos to study later. I wished I'd gotten photos of the room crammed full with antiques, but there hadn't been time.

Dorothy fussed around in her kitchen on the other side of the door, likely waiting for me. She sure seemed like a person who had something to hide, now that I was poking around.

I flushed the toilet and ran the tap for a few seconds for good measure and then opened the door. Dorothy Gallagher was right on the other side.

"Oh!" I slapped a hand to my chest as though surprised to see her there. "Those are lovely green ornaments." I pointed to the two perched on the shelf behind her toilet. "Where did you get them?"

She waved a hand and led me back to the living room. "Oh, I'm afraid I couldn't tell you. I've had those figurines for years."

Alex stood near a hutch on a side wall, making notes when we entered.

"I'm so sorry to have interrupted the flow of things," I said. But Alex didn't look annoyed with me. If anything, he looked grateful, and I wondered if he'd discovered a secret in her living room while he was there alone. I couldn't stop thinking about the Vaseline glass pieces I'd found around her house and the weathervane. Did her having it suggest that Cliff Barber had been selling antiques to Dorothy? Perhaps the hefty fees he'd been charging her were the reason for her financial troubles.

Then again, her jumpiness at me poking around suggested perhaps she had an idea that some of her items were stolen.

"Well, I just hope I can help you get to the bottom of this, although I can't imagine how I'll be of any help," Dorothy said, and then she whispered the word, "Murder," again and shook her head.

"You may not be able to." Alex used the casual relaxing tone he was so good at, which immediately made both me and Dorothy sink into living room chairs and let out a breath. "But as always, we need to get a full picture of the situation, and since you were close by here and the only one to see Miss Havenshack enter the house across the street, there's always a possibility that you might have seen something you didn't even know was important." Alex was masterful at getting suspects to relax.

"I'll certainly help if I can. Now, what, specifically, were you hoping I might have seen?"

Alex tilted his head, which I recognized as him about to get serious. "I'm not sure it's so much about what you saw. It may be more about what you said."

"Said?" She pulled back. "I never said a word to that woman." There was distaste in Dorothy's voice. Whether or not she had actually met Stella

Havenshack before, she had a clear dislike for the woman.

"Not to her." Alex drew out the last word. It certainly added drama to his next question. "We were wondering what you may have said to Cliff Barber the day before yesterday?"

Her eyes widened. "Cliff?" She swallowed, but Alex didn't fill in the silence. He let it hang there until she was ready to say more. "Did he say I spoke to him recently?" She kept her eyes on Alex, as if trying to read him like her morning newspaper.

Alex didn't answer her straight out. Instead, he said, "I went to the hospital to visit Cliff Barber yesterday."

She looked between us. "What...what did he say?"

Again, Alex didn't answer her directly. "Mrs. Gallagher, can you tell us anything about some missing antique pieces from the Montrose yard?"

By her still posture, Dorothy looked to be holding her breath. "I have no idea what you're talking about."

Alex sat on the edge of the sofa and leaned in toward her. He adopted his calming tone again. "Listen, Mrs. Gallagher. I'm not looking for an antique thief at the moment. I'm looking for a murderer. If the worst you've done is collaborated to steal a few antiques, you'd be best to come clean and tell me the truth now."

I thought about mentioning the shovels I'd just seen and the rooster weathervane. But Alex had told me to follow his lead, so I nibbled the inside of my lip to keep quiet and let the tension stretch out between them.

Dorothy took a long breath and pushed it out through pursed lips. She looked at her lap when she said, "I'm serious about antiques, and when people don't appreciate them, when people just leave them *outdoors*, I can't help myself. I have to rescue them." She said the words as though she truly believed antiques were like tiny children who had to be rescued from the Big Bad Wolf.

"And how, exactly, did you rescue them, Mrs. Gallagher?"

Dorothy slapped her lap. "He left many of them out year-round, for goodness sake! He clearly didn't care about them, and so I asked Cliff to sneak in and get a few for me." She looked between me and Alex. "But that hasn't happened for weeks, certainly not this last weekend, so what does this have to do with the poor woman who was killed?"

I, for one, was stunned by her admitting this information. I'd thought of Dorothy as a sweet older woman who was a little on the quirky side. I even thought that Cliff may have talked her into buying some of Ben's antiques and avoiding the conversation of where they had come from. I certainly hadn't anticipated that she had *asked* him to break into Ben's yard to get them for her.

And Alex had gotten all of this information out of her without her even knowing that Cliff hadn't said a word to him.

"And so you had Mr. Barber assist in that on a regular basis?" Alex asked. "How long has this been going on? And how did you convince him to help you? I understand he is not big into antiques himself."

Dorothy patted the side of her hair, her eyes still firmly planted on her lap. It took her a long time to form her answer, but when she did, her words were slow and careful. "Cliff Barber did not have a penchant for antiques, no, but he had a penchant for the freezer full of meat Ben kept for his tiger. I told Cliff I'd keep quiet about his thieving as long as helped me rescue a few treasures before they were ruined by the elements. I only wanted one a week! That's all."

I remembered her talking about how she and her husband used to shop for an antique each week. It had been an important excursion for her. I'll bet with bills piling up and having never worked, this was her way of at least solving that problem. Although, I was willing to bet if Dorothy got herself set up on Craigslist, she could make enough to live on from all the expensive old items in her house.

If she could ever part with them.

I watched Alex. He kept his eyes steady on her as he spoke. "How long has he been helping you steal?"

"Maybe six months. I think it was last summer. Ben had left his side gate open, so I saw Cliff sneaking back toward his yard with an armful of brown-wrapped meat packages. I'd been pining over one particular set of baroque garden chairs since a neighborhood barbecue Ben had put on a year or two before. I knew their absence would never have gone unnoticed when Roberta lived with Ben, but after she left, I doubted he'd even care."

"And so whenever you noticed Ben was gone, you would call Cliff and tell him to slip over and steal something from the yard?"

"He was over there helping himself to Ben's freezer full of meat anyway," she said, as though that made up for it.

"And everything he stole was from outside?"

Dorothy squirmed her shoulders. "I—sometimes he went into the house."

Alex nodded, as though he already knew this much as well. "And you knew the alarm code? Or did Cliff?"

"I found it out and gave it to Cliff."

"How did you find it out?"

I leaned forward in my chair. It was like watching a suspense flick, and I couldn't wait to hear her answers.

Dorothy put her hands over her face, clearly embarrassed. "I watched him with binoculars." She pointed across the street. "His alarm panel is straight through that window."

Alex stood and looked out Dorothy's big front window, across at the Montrose mansion. "You could see that from here?"

She nodded, face in her hands again.

"And he took everything straight back to his yard and house?" Alex assumed the answer and went on. "And he'd bring the antiques over to you and you kept these antiques for yourself?"

"Of course! No one else would appreciate them the way I would."

I agreed with her there. I'd tell Alex all about her hoarding tendencies later.

"Do you believe Cliff may have been over in the Montrose yard to steal meat for himself on Sunday, and that's when he noticed the tiger attack?"

Dorothy's eyes flitted back and forth over Alex's for a few seconds. Then her face brightened. "Yes, that must be it! That must be what happened."

"But you weren't aware of that trip?" Alex asked.

"Why, no. I had no idea." She shook her head to emphasize her point. She'd said earlier that he hadn't stolen for her in weeks, but I wasn't sure I believed that. With the way she'd spoken about the tradition she'd shared with her husband, I had a hard time believing that if she'd found a way to relive it and no one was any the wiser, she would have simply stopped.

Alex made some notes in his file. I kept my eyes on Dorothy, trying to read her level of compliance. When Alex looked up again, he changed subjects. "Walk me through this again, please, Mrs.

Gallagher."

"Dorothy," she corrected.

"Dorothy. Please tell me again exactly what you saw or heard Sunday. Don't leave anything out."

She started with noticing Stella arrive, walk down the street from her car, and go into the Montrose mansion.

"And at first you had thought it was Roberta Montrose?" Alex asked.

"Yes, yes, you're right, I did."

"And when you noticed it wasn't Roberta, you took out your phone to call Ben at his office?"

She nodded. "I used the rotary dial phone in my kitchen."

"That's the only telephone you have?" Alex asked. "You don't have a cell phone?"

"Oh, I have one. My Marvin insisted on it. But I rarely use the thing. I think it's in my purse somewhere. Technology is what is ruining our world, if you ask me."

So she wouldn't be getting rich on Craigslist anytime soon.

Alex confirmed the phone number of both her home rotary dial phone and her cell phone, made a note, but then seemed satisfied with that information. "When is the last time you visited the Montrose mansion?" he asked.

She took in a long breath and looked up to the ceiling as though she might find the answer there. "Oh, well, let me see. Maybe a month ago, I helped

Cliff bring an antique bar cart from the backyard."
She nodded at Alex, now assured, and also not
looking nearly as embarrassed about her theft. In
fact, she looked almost justified. "Look, officer, it
all happened a long time ago. I don't know why
any of this is important, or why you're not spending your time focusing on Ben Montrose. If anyone
is responsible for his girlfriend's death, it's clearly
him!"

Alex remained calm, even through her impassioned speech. "I can assure you, I have spoken to
Mr. Montrose as well as several others pertinent to
the case." Alex stood. "Thank you for your help,
Ms. Gallagher. I'll let you get back to whatever you
were doing, but I assure you, I will get to the bottom of whoever was responsible for Stella Havenshack's death. You can count on that."

Chapter Nineteen

I was so rattled by Alex's final words to Dorothy Gallagher, I followed him to his car, forgetting momentarily I had left my own car down the block.

Alex was on top of it, though. Even though I'd gotten in on his passenger side, he backed out of the driveway and pulled slowly up alongside my Prius. "Where are you meeting Amber?"

"What?" At the mention of her name, I suddenly remembered Amber's presence here, and the fact that her coming along was supposed to be a secret.

I pulled out my phone and frantically started texting. We'd spent much longer in the Gallagher house than I'd anticipated.

<Sorry! Just got out. Where should I meet you?>

When I looked up, Alex's raised eyebrows met me. "I saw her out a side window while you had Dorothy out of the room. What made you think bringing Amber and leaving her out in the cold by herself was a good idea?"

I cringed apologetically. "It was her idea. Besides, she wasn't alone."

Alex dropped one eyebrow, which meant he could read my excuse perfectly. He nodded. "She brought Hunch."

Out of pure embarrassment, I changed the subject. "Do you really think that quirky little old lady had something to do with Stella's death?"

Alex looked away. "It doesn't matter what I think. It matters what I can prove. Even if Dorothy Gallagher had motive. If she wanted Ben's antiques and heard the argument over Roberta's ring, that might have been enough to send her across the street after Stella. She may have had opportunity. I'm just not sure she had the means. She's a frail woman. Stella Havenshack had to have been half a foot taller and outweighed her by maybe twenty pounds. If Stella was terrified of animals, could Dorothy have forced her into the tiger enclosure?"

What Alex said made a lot of sense. "But if she had Cliff helping her—"

"Would she have been able to convince him to maliciously kill somebody over some frozen meat? It just doesn't seem like he has much motive in this."

Only a second later, a knock sounded on the back trunk of Alex's car. He looked into his side-view mirror, rolled down his window, and said, "Get in, kiddo."

She wasn't crazy about being called kiddo, but she got in nevertheless.

"I hear Mallory thought it was a good idea to

take you out of school for the day. Again." Alex was too good at interviewing murder suspects, so it was sometimes hard to tell when he was joking, but then he reached to the backseat, flicked off the hood of Amber's jacket, and ruffled her auburn hair. "Should we go to Velma's Donuts and talk over the case?"

Amber's eyes lit up on the word "donuts," but I looked down at his small file folder.

My brow furrowed. "Aren't all your notes at your place? We could just meet there."

Now he was the one with the furrowed brow. "These are all my notes on this case right here."

"But...you had a whole bunch of files and papers on your table last night." I'd gone back and forth about whether the papers had something to do with that beautiful blonde, but had finally convinced myself that with a big case in the works, they more likely had to do with this.

"Papers?" He shook his head as though he didn't recognize the word. "Everything is right here."

Amber cooed over Hunch in the back, but for some reason, I couldn't seem to let this go.

"You know. The papers on your kitchen table? The ones you didn't want us to see?" Now, suddenly, I was sure they had something to do with the blonde, and even though we had more important things to discuss, I was like a dog with a bone and couldn't seem to pull my teeth out of this conversation. "Or were those to do with a case for that woman?"

"Woman?" Again with the one-word question and blank expression as though I wasn't speaking English.

"The woman! The gorgeous woman that was at your townhouse last night! Taryn, was it?"

Amber opened her car door. "Can I have your keys, Mallory? I'll go warm up your car." That's what started to clue me in that I was acting crazy.

I tried to hide my blush by digging my keys out of my pocket and passing them over the seat. Amber and Hunch were gone in a flash. But before I could fully regain my composure, Alex finally spoke. "Taryn? No, Taryn wasn't there for a case. She just dropped by to pick up something of hers."

"Paperwork?" I was still stuck on this.

Alex sighed and looked across the street before turning back and meeting my eyes. "Look, Mallory, I'm sorry I was so cryptic about the paperwork on my table, but it honestly has nothing to do with this case, and it definitely doesn't have anything to do with Taryn."

My forehead buckled. I was still confused, but mostly embarrassed. I'd had issues with trust since I was a little girl, growing up with my dad always making up lies to me and my sister. As a grown woman, I felt as though I surely should be able to get past this. I crossed my arms over my chest, as if I could hide behind them.

Alex dropped his voice in that soothing way he did sometimes. He kept his multi-shaded green eyes right on me. "The papers had to do with a case I'm helping Steve with. He's been drilling into me, every time we talk, about how I have to keep all the details to myself. So I guess I was just a little hyperaware when I saw them sitting there, out in the open."

They had also been sitting out in the open while Taryn had been in his townhouse, but in an effort to contain the crazy, I pressed my lips together, so as not to mention this.

Alex looked across the street again. I suspected he was only giving me a second to calm down. "Taryn and I... we used to date, back when she lived in Honeysuckle Grove. She stopped by to pick up a few clothes she'd left at my place way back when." A blush came over his cheeks, and he kept his eyes across the street.

"Way back when?" I couldn't keep my question in.

He shook his head and finally looked at me. "It was over a year ago. I've barely heard from her since. I saw her one time at the Morgantown police headquarters when we drove there on that case."

My mind whirred. Amber and I had been walking around Morgantown, trying to find a possible suspect for a murder, oblivious to the fact that Alex had been in the police building conversing with his old flame.

The worst part was, the police captain in Morgantown had treated Alex so well, I'd been afraid he might consider a move there.

"So she came to pick up some clothes and try to convince you to make a move to Morgantown," I said, deadpan. Deep down, I knew I had to want what was best for Alex, even if it meant losing him.

But he laughed. "Believe me, moving to some college town to solve the odd drunken brawl doesn't interest me. I grew up here. I want to make my own town safe." He touched my shoulder. "*Our* own town."

Now I was the one blushing. "So you're not moving away?" I asked meekly.

He shook his head. "No plans to. And I am really sorry that I have to keep that other case from you." He glanced across the street again, so I knew he felt bad about it.

I waved a hand. "Oh, don't worry about that. Detective Reinhart has every right to tell you to keep case details from us." I motioned between me and Amber, in my car, as I didn't want to be the only one he'd been instructed to keep case details from. "At least he asks you nicely."

Alex nodded, but didn't say anything else. Honestly, I was kind of surprised he wasn't telling me how he'd argued that Amber and I had been a lot of help in the past and how we knew how to be discreet. But I inwardly hoped he had done that and he just didn't want to rehash it now.

"So Velma's Donuts?" he asked. "Not as good as your baked goods, but I'd like to go over everything while it's fresh in our minds."

As we got out of our cars at the donut shop,

Alex told Amber, "After this, Mallory will drive you back to school."

Amber ducked her head sheepishly. Alex, while not very stern with Amber, never had to tell her anything twice. She was missing a father figure in her life, and he seemed to be exactly what she needed. She knew it, too.

Thirty seconds later, we were warming up in the only donut shop in town that boasted a fireplace. Thankfully, the place was empty, other than people picking up coffee and donuts to go, so we got a table close to the fire without any fear of being overheard.

Amber had a duffel bag full of clothes she'd planned to drop off at my place and swap with the drawer full that was there, but she'd emptied it in my car to make room for Hunch. Cats weren't typically permitted in donut shops, but again, Amber felt it was better to ask for forgiveness than permission in the event that Hunch was spotted.

"What did you find out?" Alex asked Amber when we all had donuts and coffee in front of us. I'd chosen an apple fritter because it looked fresh and crunchy on the outside, but I wasn't kidding myself. Chances were good it would sit here untouched if we were discussing a case.

"Nothing in the Gallagher yard." She took a big bite of her éclair, stuffed on one side with cream and custard. We waited while she chewed and swallowed. "But Cliff Barber's place had pretty easy access to my Uncle Ben's backyard."

We listened as she went on about a gate that looked like it latched and locked, but it had actually been augmented with black electrician's tape, so it only took a little shove to get open.

"His backyard was pretty neglected. Even though we haven't had snow in a few days, none of the snow was worn down with footprints, except for a small path toward the back gate that separated his yard from my uncle's yard."

Alex nodded and made a note, but we had already established that Cliff had made the trek over to the Montrose yard two days ago. We just didn't know why yet.

"Would you be able to tell if the footprints in Cliff's yard match the ones near the tiger enclosure?" I asked.

Alex shook his head. "With the amount of rain we've had, it's not likely." Alex made another note. "There was enough wet carpet and flooring inside the mansion that our forensics team suspected two or even three people of traipsing through the house in wet boots. The water spots decreased on the stairway, but went all the way to the bedroom."

"Maybe Dorothy told Cliff to go after the ring? Maybe she knew Stella was in the mansion and hoped Cliff could overtake her once she found the ring?"

Alex took the last bite of his honey crueler before going back to his notes.

"So Dorothy called him when she saw Stella

entering the mansion," Amber started, launching into a possible scenario as though she could see it happening before her. "Told him to meet her in Uncle Ben's backyard. They came up with the idea to throw Stella into the tiger's cage, and then chased her throughout the mansion until they grabbed her?"

Alex twisted his lips. Something about the scenario still wasn't sitting right with me, either. "Again, there's not a lot of motive to kill her, especially in such a brutal way."

"Can you check Dorothy's phone records to see if she made a call to Cliff around that time in the afternoon?"

Alex nodded and pulled out his phone. "That I can do." He made a quick quiet call to the police department.

"Ow!" Amber looked down at her duffel bag. "Stop it, Hunchie," she hissed quietly.

But when I looked down, Hunch's little paw reached out to claw her leg again.

"Are you forgetting anything?" I asked Amber. "Did Hunch find anything in the Gallagher yard or Cliff Barber's yard?" In my experience, Hunch only clawed one of us when we were missing a crucial bit of information.

Amber scowled, but only for a second. Then enlightenment eased onto her face. She reached in her coat pocket and pulled out a Ziploc baggie with something green inside.

"Vaseline glass?" I asked.

Amber nodded. "After so many people going through the backyard and the rain, most of the snow was gone in my uncle's backyard. Hunch found another shard of it near the entrance to the tiger enclosure."

We showed it to Alex as soon as he sat down again.

"I snapped pictures with my phone and left a twig to mark the spot, but I figured you'd need to take it in to prove it's a match," Amber told him proudly.

But Alex only nodded, took the item, and said, "Thanks," as though it wasn't all that important.

"Everything okay?" I asked.

He nodded. After a pause, he said, "Yeah, yeah. It just turns out I have to get back to the station. Mickey has some info about Carson Kroeger and he wants to tell me in person." Alex's gaze flitted out the window toward his car.

"Sure, yes, go," I told him. "We'll be fine. Besides, I should get Amber back to school."

He stood, nodded again, and turned to leave. As he headed for the door, he had his phone out and was texting someone.

As soon as he was outside, Amber said, "That was weird. What do you think this news was about Kroeger?" She bent to calm Hunch, who was getting restless.

Alex was acting strange. I watched him slip his phone away and get into his car, and right at that second, my phone buzzed in my pocket. I was about to grab for it when something stopped me.

Instead, I pulled out my car keys and slid them across the table. "Too much coffee," I told Amber, motioning to the bathroom. "I'll meet you in the car?"

Amber agreed quickly, eager to get Hunch out of the donut shop before he was spotted.

I'd barely gotten through the bathroom door when I had my phone out and my text from Alex open.

<Didn't want to say anything in front of Amber. There were fresh prints from Roberta on the green glass, and on the glasses in the master bedroom. Not only that, but hers were a match for the prints on the back gate. Get Amber to school or at least keep her busy. Mickey and I are meeting at the flower shop. I'll update you when I can.>

When I put my phone away, I was holding my breath. How was I going to tell Amber if Alex had to arrest her aunt on charges of murder?

Chapter Twenty

I got into my car, feeling especially shaky about trying to keep something so big from Amber, but thankfully, her attention stayed on my cat. Hunch was perched on his hind legs on her lap and having another eye-to-eye discussion with her.

"Should we go talk to Chad again, Hunchie? Do you think if you sniff around you'll find any more of this Vaseline glass in his store?"

I had a sneaking suspicion that if I told Amber she was going straight to school, she'd have a slew of arguments, and I'd accidentally blurt something I shouldn't. At the same time, my cat might be an investigative whiz, but I didn't trust him to pad through Chad's precarious Antique Village without breaking anything.

"I think you're right. We'll stop and talk to Chad, but Hunch is staying in the car, and then you're going straight to school, no matter what we find out." I was surprised at how self-assured my voice came out. "Helping Alex can wait until after three o'clock."

Amber didn't agree but at least she didn't

argue. "What do you think it means if Vaseline glass was found all over the yard?"

It had only been found in two places, but I didn't mention this. Instead, my mind was on Roberta and why her green glass hadn't been missing any shards.

"My Uncle Ben found Cliff in his yard, so he was definitely there that day. He could have knocked Stella on the head with some antique made with Vaseline glass. Once she was knocked out, he would've been able to get her into the tiger's cage without getting hurt himself," she suggested, but she still hadn't come up with a motive of why Cliff would have done this. "Seth has a black light. I think we should get back there and look for more green glass."

The last place she should be right now was back at her uncle's house. "Alex has both shards, and we don't even know if they match yet. If he doesn't come up with anything with Kroeger, I'm sure he'll have forensics look closer at the yard." My voice was getting less self-assured by the moment, but thankfully, Amber was caught up in her theories and didn't seem to notice.

"But then why was Cliff in the mansion getting his soppy boots everywhere?"

"Stealing the ring?" I suggested, even though I didn't suspect this was the case. Now that I knew about Roberta's fingerprints, I could visualize her fighting Stella throughout the house. I wondered if Roberta had the ring now. She must, but she hadn't been wearing it at the flower shop.

"Or there's Dorothy Gallagher. I think you should show Chad the pictures you took of the antiques in her house."

I'd shown Amber and Alex these in the donut shop. I had wanted Alex to look into the solvent I found in Dorothy's back room, but now perhaps that wouldn't be necessary. Still, I was glad to have Amber's attention on the two neighbors.

"And that Dorothy lady did have her own Vaseline glass," Amber went on.

"You're right," I said, driving toward town. "Let's go see if Chad can help us figure this out."

Chapter Twenty-one

"One more stop, and then you're definitely going back to school," I told Amber sternly as we pulled up in front of Chad's Antique Village.

"Yes, *Mom,*" she said again, and then led the way out of the car, through the courtyard, and into the main part of Chad's shop.

"Hi, Chad," I said when we made our way through the chiming door and he continued to fiddle with his wares with his back to us.

He turned and recognition immediately crossed his face. "Little drops of heaven was right! Didya bring me any more of those little caramel delicacies?"

I smiled. "I'm afraid not today, but we're glad you enjoyed them, aren't we, Amber?"

Amber beamed.

"I need to get your recipe! Also, I wonder if you'd consider serving some of your desserts at my antique auction later this month? I hold one every New Year's Eve at the community center."

Amber and I had talked more than once about starting a catering business, ever since my dad was in town and I'd used that as an excuse with him. It wasn't a bad idea to try helping Chad out to see if we liked doing it.

"We'll definitely think about that," I hedged, "but for today, I'm afraid we have some additional questions."

"Sure. What can I help with?" Chad looked between me and Amber.

"We're just looking for a little more information on your Vaseline glass," I told Chad. Chad had left the piece out that he'd shown us the day before. "You said this was the only piece you have for sale at the moment?" I double-checked.

Chad nodded and sighed. "I could swear I used to have more. The uranium glass is popular with certain aficionados, so I pick them up when I see them at thrift marts or estate sales."

"So you haven't actually sold any lately?" Amber asked.

Chad shook his head. "Haven't sold any in years."

I pulled out my phone and navigated to the photos I'd snapped while in the Gallagher house. I started with my shots of the bathroom. It only had two Vaseline glass pieces, but I wondered if he may recognize some of the other pieces. "Do any of these antique wares look familiar?"

It only took him a second. "Yes, yes! I sold Marvin and Dot that jeweled elephant last year." He looked up at me to explain further the era it had been derived from, but I wasn't particularly interested in the jeweled elephant.

I was sad to hear that Dorothy's husband's passing was so recent. "Anything else?" I wiggled my phone screen in front of him.

He looked closer and used two fingers to zoom in, but this time, his face showed something different than recognition. "Those Vaseline glass figurines. They were here two months ago, and I've been looking for them ever since. I figured I'd misplaced them…"

Amber filled in the blank he left. "Could you have sold them and not remembered? Or could one of your employees have sold them?"

I looked around the small crowded room, as though another employee might be hiding, squished among the wares.

He shook his head. "No employees, I'm afraid. It's just me. Even if my memory isn't reliable, I mark down every item I sell." He went to his computer to type something in. "The figurines are still listed in my inventory." He looked between me and Amber. "Wait, you don't think Dot stole them?"

That was exactly what I thought, although it seemed to have less to do with the case now if Roberta was guilty. Alex could deal with any theft charges once he was done with his murder case. Then again, I couldn't see Chad laying charges against the old widow. He probably just wanted his wares back.

I figured I might as well see if Chad recognized any other pieces that may have been stolen from him, mostly to keep Amber feeling like she was accomplishing something on the case.

He recognized two more pieces from Dorothy's entry and the reality of the situation was settling in on him. Dorothy—Dot—Gallagher had been visiting and getting him talking every week for months, simply so she could steal something from his store.

Again, he used two fingers to zoom in, and a second later, he looked up in astonishment. "This is Dot's house? These are all mine!"

"All of them?" Amber and I looked at each other and then back to Chad.

He zoomed in further and turned my phone to show me. "Definitely this decanter set. It's one of a kind. And the coral frame over here. And this engraved candelabra. If you had a better photo, I'd even confirm that it says '1525 Ashbury Street' along the bottom."

I took in a breath and reached for my phone, but at that second, Chad pulled it closer to his nose. "Huh. I wonder where the other piece went."

"Other piece?" Amber and I asked at once.

He turned to show me the plaque on the hutch, the one with the two hooks that looked as though it should be holding something.

"What was the other piece?" I asked.

"It was that Vaseline glass you two are asking about. It was a sword. The metal shaft of the thing rested on these two hooks, and the glass blade pointed straight down."

Chapter Twenty-two

"Could the glass sword have just fallen and broken?" I was trying to poke holes in every theory at this point. Ever since Chad revealed the missing glass piece from the plaque, I felt torn. Was Roberta Montrose truly guilty? Or could Dorothy Gallagher have played a part in Stella Havenshack's death? But she was old and frail, I reminded myself.

Then again, if she had found a way to talk Cliff Barber into helping her…

"A *Vaseline glass* sword?" Amber asked. "What are the chances? There has to be a way to prove that Dorothy Gallagher was involved."

The missing sword could have been instrumental in Stella Havenshack's death or it could be unrelated. Either way, we had to prove it.

"If she was stabbed before being thrown into the tiger's cage, and if the glass sword was broken, shouldn't there be some evidence of it in the victim's body?" Amber asked as I drove toward her school.

I nodded. "I wonder if Alex mentioned that to the coroner. Perhaps they could check her remains with a black light."

Amber picked up her phone. "I'll text Alex and suggest it."

"Why don't you wait until—"

But her thumbs flew over her phone and she cut me off, saying, "Done."

I hated to think she had just interrupted a crucial interview.

"So what's our next move?" She had to know I was driving toward the high school. Regardless, she asked, "Do we go back and put more pressure on the Gallagher woman to talk?"

"What we really need is a confirmation from forensics that the shards of glass are even a clue. Maybe they'll find some of the victim's blood on them. Or maybe the coroner will find some trace of the uranium glass. Then we'll have something, but at this point, we have to wait for Alex, and you have to go to school."

Amber let out a frustrated sigh. But she didn't argue for three more blocks.

Finally, it came out. "It's the week before Christmas break. I've already passed my courses, and once I show Mom my report card, I'll be able to do it all online next semester. And there's obviously more important stuff than English assignments right now. You have to agree." She waited for my response, but I didn't give one.

She was right, but at the same time, I still worried that Alex was going to come back with a text that he'd arrested Roberta Montrose for murder, and Amber might see it before I could break it to her gently.

Besides, she was a teenager who should be doing normal teenage things, at least some of the time. Not spending her days with almost thirty-year-olds investigating dead people.

"Couldn't you just drop me off at home then?"

"It's four hours, Amber. Let's remember that your mom's already not too happy with me, and Alex shouldn't even be involving us in these cases." I'd been extra worried about this since our conversation earlier about the papers he'd had to keep hidden from us on his table. Part of me wondered if he regretted bringing us in on this case at all. "If he thinks you should go to school and I should hang out at home and wait, that's probably the least we could do."

She didn't agree or disagree, but she did let out another frustrated huff as I pulled up to the curb near the high school. Normally, Hunch had a way of calming her down, but not today. In fact, Hunch seemed growly and irritable, probably because he was about to be separated from his bestie.

"I'll see you in four hours," she said, looking Hunch in the eye. Then she got out of the car without a word to me and headed for the school doors.

As I pulled away, I talked to Hunch. "I know, I know, you're mad at me, too, right? But we don't always get to do what we want in life, Hunch, do we?"

He perched on his hind legs, looking out my

passenger window, and didn't pay a lick of attention to my rant.

"It's only four hours. Seriously, what's the big —"

My words were cut off by Hunch's low, guttural growl. Hunch wasn't much of a squirrel chaser. In fact, not much in nature interested him. However, plenty in the investigative world interested him.

I looked out his window. "What? What do you see?" I wondered if Dorothy Gallagher was wandering around this part of town, on some sort of antique hunt. "Is it to do with the case?"

Another growl greeted me, this one louder, and he kept his gaze fixated in the direction of the street past the high school. I had nowhere pressing to be, and since my cat couldn't speak English to let me know if he truly saw something of importance, I decided to make a quick right and follow his senses.

No sooner had I turned the corner than I knew exactly what he'd been growling at. Amber was just stepping up onto a city bus.

"What on earth...?"

Hunch didn't have much to say on the subject until the bus pulled away. Then he let out another growl.

"Uh, yeah," I said, suddenly indignant. "You bet I'm going to follow her."

I held back a few car lengths, in case Amber was looking out the window. If she knew she was being followed, I had no doubt her speedy teenage brain would have no problem giving us the slip.

"Easier to ask forgiveness than permission," I muttered as I drove. I'd always figured she had no problem using the expression for others, and especially her mom, but we trusted each other. Didn't we?

When the city bus started climbing a hill out of town, I knew exactly where it was headed.

"She didn't want to go to school so badly that she'd sneak away to go home? How's she going to explain that to her mom?" My question wasn't a real one, and Hunch didn't even spare me a glance with it. In truth, Helen Montrose probably wouldn't even notice her youngest child arriving home four hours early.

As I followed the bus at a distance, I wondered if Amber might be avoiding something or someone at school that she hadn't been able to tell me about. It wouldn't be the first time she'd felt social tensions. Maybe after her mom's strange birthday party, teenagers from school had been acting weird around her. Or maybe she worried that someone would have heard about her Uncle Ben getting arrested and the death on his property.

I slowed, nearing the Montrose mansion, but held back a good half block. Sure enough, Amber skipped down the bus steps and across the street, oblivious to where I was half-hidden across the street behind a Land Rover. Seconds later, she slipped through the front door into her house.

I turned my phone over in my hands. "I don't get it, Hunch? Why won't she talk to me? Should I text her?"

Hunch remained rapt on where Amber had disappeared. I heaved in a few deep breaths and let them out, remunerating, but finally decided to put my car into gear.

Another growl from Hunch made me stop, just as I was about to hit the gas. I looked up and there was Amber again. She wore a blue knapsack on her back, and she jogged down the street in the other direction, away from us.

I edged my car forward to keep her in view, and seconds later, she stopped and sat at a bus stop on the other side of the road.

I quickly darted behind another car along the curb. Her gaze stayed on her phone, and I wondered if I had accidentally texted her when I had been considering it. Or perhaps she felt guilty about ditching school and texted me to let me know she was headed back there.

But by the time the bus arrived from the other direction and Amber boarded, I had zero new text messages.

I ducked as the bus sailed past me, and even Hunch seemed to know to jump onto the car floor for thirty seconds. Then I put my car in reverse, spun around, and followed the bus.

At the bottom of the hill I affectionately referred to as Montrose Mountain, I was surprised to see the bus take a right turn, away from the high school, and also not anywhere near the direction of my house.

"Where is she going?" I asked Hunch.

Hunch's low growl sounded like he was as much in the dark as I was, but somehow he knew something was wrong. Hunch had a sixth sense in general, but especially when it came to his best friend. She was my best friend, too, but apparently, I wasn't nearly as intuitive. Only a moment ago, I'd been certain that Amber felt guilty for lying and was headed back for school.

As the bus headed out of town, the route became familiar. I'd traveled it three times in the last three days. Amber was headed to her uncle's mansion.

That, or the Gallagher home full of antiques, or maybe even Cliff Barber's place.

"What does she think she's going to accomplish out here by herself?"

Hunch's growl reminded me that she wasn't by herself. At least Hunch had been observant enough to make certain of that.

Sure enough, the bus pulled over a block from the other Montrose mansion. I sailed by it. Now that I knew where she was headed, I could park somewhere out of sight, head to her uncle's mansion, and confront her.

In truth, I was as frustrated as she was about having to wait for answers from Alex on this one. And as I reconsidered the situation, I figured if we stayed out of sight, and this kept us busy for the

DENISE JADEN

next couple of hours while Alex interviewed Roberta Montrose, why shouldn't we?

Of course, Amber and Hunch had already
combed over all three properties earlier today.
Plus, the forensics team had thoroughly investigated Ben's yard. But I wanted to believe Amber
hadn't come out here without a plan.

Hunch wasn't about to let me leave him in the
car, despite how much he hated getting his paws
wet and cold, and I had no problem with that.
I hoped he would admonish Amber with a few
growls before he snuggled up to her, which I knew
he eventually would.

I didn't want to confront her out in the
neighborhood, where Dorothy Gallagher would no
doubt be watching, so I snuck down the side yard
of Cliff Barber's house, through his backyard, and
over to the gate that separated his yard from Ben
Montrose's. Sure enough, the mechanism had been
taped with electrical tape so it wouldn't click shut.

I found a crime scene marker at the base of the
gate. Careful not to touch it, I pulled on some latex
gloves before nudging the gate open.

Amber knelt on the snow-flecked ground
about fifty feet away, extracting something from
her backpack. She was another twenty feet from
the tiger enclosure where Boots paced and growled
in her direction, covering any noise I might have
made. I remembered what Roberta Montrose had
mentioned about letting the tiger miss a few
meals, but Amber barely seemed to notice the big

cat, driven to her task. When I saw the item she'd brought, I knew her plan immediately. It was a black light, along with an extra-long yellow extension cord.

She'd gone home to pick it up Seth's black light to search for more green glass herself.

My phone buzzed in my pocket, and even though I knew it couldn't be Amber texting me, it could be Alex, so I silently pulled the gate shut and backed into Cliff's yard to check it.

Usually, Alex texted, so I figured a voicemail meant it was important. I quickly plugged in my voicemail code to check it.

"Mallory, it's me." His voice sounded frustrated, or maybe even angry. "Once we put some pressure on her and got Roberta Montrose talking, she admitted she had been at the mansion on Sunday. She was up in the master bedroom and had just found her wedding ring when she heard voices from the bottom of the stairs. She took the ring and the glass, so Ben would know right away that she'd found it, and headed down a rear stairway that led to the backyard. She said she could only recognize one of the voices as Stella's. The other one was quieter and female."

"Dorothy Gallagher," I whispered aloud, just before Alex suggested the same name.

"Mickey and I are going to drive by Dorothy Gallagher's house. There's something not sitting right about her stolen antiques and the solvent you mentioned. Oh, and I just stopped by the hospital to talk to Cliff, and would you believe they released him? He wasn't well enough to give a statement yesterday, but apparently, he'd made a *miraculous* recovery and checked himself out this morning. I insisted upon talking to his doctor—"

I was so caught up in listening to Alex's rant that I didn't notice the bulky figure before me until it said, "Drop the phone and keep your hands where I can see them."

Chapter Twenty-three

"I—I just have to—" I tried to come up with an excuse of why I couldn't drop my phone right this second, but Cliff Barber cocked the handgun he had aimed straight at my head.

That helped me make the decision, and I tossed my cell phone gently to the ground, Alex's voicemail still quietly murmuring through it.

"You people have to keep snooping around, don't you?" Cliff Barber had looked much friendlier on his Facebook profile. Up close, he seemed a combination of dangerous and fearful. He loomed above me, at least six-four, and his long-sleeve T-shirt stretched tight over muscular arms. I remembered him having some kind of condition where he saw himself as small or weak, but I found that hard to believe.

His teeth gritted together with tension, his black eyebrows knit together, and the gun trembled in his hand.

I wasn't sure what to say to his question, nor what he meant by "you people." Did that mean he had heard from Dorothy that I'd been asking questions with Alex? Or did it mean he'd already spotted Amber snooping around his neighbor's yard?

"I just—my cat got loose out here some-where," I said, the only ready excuse I could come up with. In truth, I had no idea where Hunch had disappeared to. Had he gone into the Montrose yard while I had the gate open? Or was he lurking in a bush somewhere nearby, watching his owner get threatened at gunpoint?

"Your cat?" Cliff's deep unbelieving voice rat-tled me. He didn't sound like someone who had re-cently needed hospitalization. I still suspected he'd played up being much more injured and trauma-tized than he actually was to avoid police question-ing. "Why don't you tell it to the caged monster next door?"

My mouth went dry. If Cliff had indeed been the one to throw Stella Havenshack into the tiger enclosure, apparently, he had no reservations with throwing a second woman in there.

"No!" I shouted, hoping Amber would hear me over Boots's loud growls. "You might have thrown Stella Havenshack in with the tiger, but you won't get me in there without a fight!"

But a second later, Dorothy Gallagher's voice sounded from across the fence. "Get over here, Cliff. I need you to take care of this little sneak!"

"I've got my own little sneak over here." Cliff came closer and nudged me toward the gate with the muzzle of his gun. When we got close, he kicked the gate open using more force than he needed to. It made a *thwack* sound as it hit the fence.

And then my mouth went dry for another reason. Dorothy Gallagher had Amber's yellow extension cord wrapped around her wrists, ankles, and neck, so tightly I could see it digging in from here.

She lay on the wet grass with her eyes closed, and I couldn't even tell if she was conscious.

Chapter Twenty-four

Dorothy Gallagher must have snuck up behind Amber while she was concentrating on her work with the black light. Otherwise, I couldn't see any way that the slight woman could have overtaken Amber, who had to be stronger in body and was most definitely stronger in spirit.

"Give me the gun," Dorothy instructed Cliff in a tone that sounded more like a parent than a neighbor. "I'll keep an eye on Mrs. Beck while you get rid of this one." She motioned her chin to Amber on the ground.

"Oh, no, you won't!" I rushed toward Amber. Who cared what that meant for me. I had to make sure she was okay! I had to somehow prevent these people from feeding my best friend to a starved tiger.

But Dorothy called out, "Hit her, Cliff! Use all that manly strength!"

And a second later, a blunt force hit the side of my head. I collapsed to the ground in pain not far from Amber and let out a moan.

In that second, I realized that whether Amber was conscious or not, she probably had chosen well to play unconscious. I kept my eyes closed so I could take a minute to gather my strength.

"Deal with the Beck woman first," Dorothy instructed from above me. "I don't think this other one's going to wake up, and if she does, I'll just tug nice and tight on this cord."

I tried to keep still at her words and not react, even though my heart was beating a thousand times a minute.

"I…can't," a wimpy voice said from above me.

"You *can*!" Dorothy commanded him. "You're so strong, Cliff. Look at those muscles poking out of your shirt. You're like Hercules!"

"But I never meant to hurt anybody," he whined. "I should just talk to the police."

Dorothy Gallagher laughed. "Do you think they'll believe you had no idea there was a woman wrapped up in that carpet? They'll say there's no way you could have believed a carpet was that heavy!"

"But you said it was made from rabbit skins."

Dorothy laughed again. "They're not going to believe your innocent act. I'm sure you knew all along what you were doing, and when you go to prison, I'll bet all those other men are going to just think your muscles are extra special."

Her taunting voice got to him. "I can't go to prison! You can't let that happen!"

I was torn between opening my eyes and telling Cliff I was on his side and would talk to the police for him, and playing passed out to gather my strength for a few more seconds.

"I won't let that happen, Cliff." Her voice sounded motherly again. "You do what you know has to be done here, and we'll take care of each other. Nobody has to go to prison over this."

A second later, I felt his arms underneath me, lifting me up. I tried my best to go limp, but all the while, my mind whirred for ideas. I could tell when we were nearing the tiger enclosure by the volume and intensity of Boots's growls. It took everything in me to stay still, and I murmured quietly, hoping Dorothy would no longer be able to hear my words.

"If you tell the truth, the police will believe you. I know them. I'll tell them everything you said."

"Don't listen to her, Cliff!" Dorothy wasn't far enough away. "She's friends with the police and they have to find someone to take the fall for this."

I tried to yell and overtake Dorothy's words, but after Cliff's knock to my skull, my head throbbed with each sound I made. My words held no power. It felt like blowing into a hurricane.

"You know you can trust me," Dorothy barreled on. "You know you can believe what I say. You were strong enough to throw Stella in there, and you're strong enough for this!"

Cliff moved forward again, and I was spent from trying to yell. I had no more ideas and not enough strength to overtake him, at least not while Dorothy was around building him up.

My body jostled as he moved quickly with me

to the gate of the tiger enclosure. Boots growled loudly and banged the inner gate as he saw us approach. I kicked and clawed at Cliff, bit his shoulder and scratched his arms, using every bit of my strength, but he seemed to barely notice my fight. He typed in the code for the gate, and a second later, a long beep sounded.

And then the automatic gate clicked open.

Only a second after that, I was down on the ground again, but this time on the concrete pad between the two gates. Boots loomed at the inner one, frothing at the mouth.

Cliff backed out of the outer gate, ready to lock me in and open the bars that separated me from one very hungry tiger. I clawed at his feet and his ankles, trying to yank myself back onto the grass, but he hit the control pad, kicked me back with his strong leg, and the outer gate shut between us.

The inner gate clicked and started to open. This was it for me. But I'd much rather lose my life than someone else I loved.

Please, God. Find a way to help Amber!

Chapter Twenty-five

"Dorothy Gallagher! Drop the gun!"

I was only relieved at the sound of Alex's voice for one second. And then Boots's paw swiped only inches from my leg through the opening of the inner gate.

Alex could at least save Amber, I reasoned in an instant. I'd die a horrible death, but I'd at least do it knowing Amber would be safe. I pushed back against the outer gate and pulled both legs to my chest. My breath came out in quick staccato and my heart pounded.

A second later, a gunshot rang out and what sounded like a male exclamation of pain. I couldn't tell if Cliff or Alex, but if it wasn't Dorothy, I had to deduce she'd shot Alex.

Nooooooo! my brain screamed.

But I had my own problems. Boots worked his large, sharp claws closer toward me through the widening space of the sliding inner gate. I had already backed myself as close to the outer gate as humanly possible. I slapped my hands around in every direction and knocked over a metal pole. It had a hook on the end and was the one I'd seen

Carson Kroeger carrying after he's subdued Boots on Sunday. Without thinking twice, I jammed it toward the tiger's paw. This backed him up, but only for the briefest of seconds. Then it made him angrier, and he swatted at the pole.

It wouldn't be a fair fight. The slight bit of metal would be no match for Boots once he could squeeze through the opening. But the metal pole was collapsible. After pushing in a pin, it could fold into what looked like three sections. I looked toward the track of the inner gate and the space it had left to travel. With a sudden idea and with shaking hands, I collapsed one of the pins and jammed the section of pole into the back end of the track.

Before I could collapse the other section to add some strength, the gate stuttered and made a loud buzzing sound as it tried again to open. It closed a couple of inches and tried to open again. The pole bent a little, but held it back, at least for the moment. It wouldn't last forever, though. I had to get out of the small safety enclosure, and fast.

I scrambled to my feet. There was a keypad for the gates in here, but I couldn't see the card with the code on the other side of the outer gate, and I couldn't for the life of me remember it. Was there an eight in it? A three?

I looked up, but even if I could have climbed the cross-hatch fence, razor wire lined the top on every side. Any other time, I might have been thankful for the measures Ben Montrose had put in place to keep his tiger secure, but not now.

The pole jammed in the track let out a metallic groan as the gate pushed against it once again.

Another gunshot fired. I'd already been so heartbroken that Alex had been shot and might not be able to save Amber. This one surprised me so much, I shrieked without meaning to.

"You can get them!" Dorothy said, through what sounded like gritted teeth. "Pull it together, Cliff! You can help me take them all."

"Quiet!" Alex yelled. "Stay back." I suspected his words were aimed at Cliff, but I couldn't tell from here. "Amber—hurry, go let Mallory out!"

Amber was conscious? But before I could rejoice over the sound of the outer door clicking open, the pole on the inner door buckled and the gate slid the rest of the way open.

I was face to face with a very large, very hungry tiger.

Chapter Twenty-six

Amber grasped my arm through the outer door's opening. Before I knew what was happening, Hunch raced past me. It was enough to distract Boots, at least for a second, and he turned his head to watch Hunch race through his enclosure. Then he leapt after my cat, apparently more eager for a chase than a full human meal.

My mind had trouble catching up, but Amber yanked me toward the larger opening. She slapped the control to shut the door, and it didn't seem to move fast enough, but at least it closed before Boots directed his attention back to us.

"Are you two okay?" Alex didn't take his eyes from the figures in front of him. Through the opening in his jacket, I could see a growing splotch of blood staining his light-blue shirt between his neck and his shoulder. I sucked in a breath.

Dorothy huddled in pain, grasping her arm. Cliff rocked in a ball on the ground with his hands over his ears, murmuring, "I can't kill anyone! I can't!"

"We're okay," I huffed out. "Thanks to Hunch."

At the thought, I scrambled around the side of

the tiger enclosure so I could see inside. It wasn't hard to locate my cat, as Boots was on his hind legs, clawing at the base of the tallest, thinnest tree in the enclosure.

"You stay right there, Hunchie," Amber called to him. "Don't worry, Boots can't climb a tree that skinny. We'll get you."

Alex instructed me to grab the handcuffs from where they were hooked to his belt and secure Cliff. "Amber, take my keys and get another pair from my trunk, please."

Amber took one last glance at Hunch and then jogged toward the front yard, looking no worse for wear for all she had been through today.

By the time Alex had Dorothy and Cliff secured and two other officers had arrived to take them away, I was spent.

But there was still the matter of rescuing my heroic cat.

Chapter Twenty-seven

Alex called Carson Kroeger in, saying he would put in a good word with the judge about the bribes he'd been taking if he double-timed it to the Montrose mansion to sedate Boots for a few hours.

Even with Alex's good words, an internal investigation had already been launched into the bribes Carson Kroeger had been accepting and how Ben Montrose had gotten a permit for a tiger in the first place.

Hunch didn't have much patience for the fireman who finally hitched up a ladder and rescued him from the tallest tree within the tiger enclosure, but at least his claws couldn't permeate the heavy fire suit.

The fireman tried to pass Hunch to me, but I motioned to Amber. After the trauma they'd both endured today, I figured they needed each other.

Alex had to wait for Animal Control to arrive from upstate. He'd called them once after Stella's death, but at that time, it had appeared as a one-time freak accident. With more danger today involving the same tiger, Alex had called it in as an emergency. Ben Montrose would have to prove his ability to keep people safe from his tiger to get him back, even temporarily, but Animal Control said that wasn't likely to happen, no matter how much money Ben Montrose tried to throw at the problem. Stan at the wildlife reserve would be relieved.

We planned to meet Alex back at my place after he had tied up the details. As soon as Amber and I walked in the door, Hunch practically leapt for his food dish and devoured the whole thing in what seemed like two gulps.

"I'll bet you're hungry, my little hero."

Hunch waited patiently as I refilled his dish.

I turned to Amber. "You know what I need? A long, hot shower. You okay if I go do that?" I didn't think she was too shaken up from today, but figured I'd better check.

"Go for it," she said. She headed for my living room. "I'm just going to lie down for a few."

When I came downstairs after my shower, both Amber and Hunch were out cold on my couch. I tiptoed past them to the kitchen and tried to be as quiet as possible when opening my freezer. I didn't have the energy for cooking, but I'd been saving a special treat for one day when we felt a little more celebratory.

I also grabbed a bottle of sparkling apple juice from the pantry and put it in the fridge to chill.

Alex often knocked and then came right in, but today he rang the doorbell, which woke up Amber and Hunch. I hurried to the door, as though I could turn back time and the sound of the doorbell. I found Alex out on my porch, leaning against the wall like he could barely hold himself upright.

I rushed out to him. After all, he'd been shot today.

"Oh, Alex! Come in. Are you okay?" My heart ratcheted up all over again as I remembered the gunshot ringing out. "Have you been to the hospital?"

He chuckled. "I'm good. I've been looked at, and Dorothy's bullet just grazed me." He slipped out of his coat inside my entry and showed me the square white bandage near his clavicle.

Still, I couldn't help seeing the growing splotch of blood that had been there. I couldn't help imagining the bullet hitting him a deadly few inches over. The fact that he'd been shot in the line of duty today rattled me to no end. "Are you sure?"

He circled an arm around me and squeezed me in a side hug. "I'm sure. Just exhausted."

"I bet."

By the time we went to the kitchen, Amber stood near my table with Hunch in her arms. "What's this?"

I grinned. "Your *real* birthday party."

I'd only had time to blow up three balloons,

but I had my pink lemonade cupcakes thawed and laid out, along with champagne glasses and other nibbles from my freezer. There was also a gift wrapped up at Amber's usual seat at the table.

She bit back a smile as she sat in front of it. Sometimes, I thought of her as almost as mature as me and Alex. Other times, like this, she really was a giddy teenager.

"Go ahead." I motioned with my chin. "Open it."

She tore at the wrapping and seconds later, held up the purple hoodie I'd had made for her. It declared: HOME IS WHERE THE CAT IS.

"It really is." She snuggled Hunch onto her lap and wrapped him in her new hoodie.

We spent the rest of the evening decompressing and talking over case details as we always did. With the confession Alex had talked out of Cliff, he had already pieced most of it together.

"I guess the argument Ben and Roberta had on Saturday evening put everything in motion," he said. "Ben had a way of taunting the women in his life, and by the time Roberta left, he had made Roberta, Stella, and Dorothy across the street all desperate for the antique ring."

"But Roberta was the only one who knew where to find it?" I suggested.

Alex nodded. "You're probably right. Stella had likely been following Roberta, waiting for her to come back for the ring. But Stella never made it upstairs to confront Roberta because Dorothy was suddenly threatening her with a green glass sword."

"So did Dorothy actually go over to my uncle's mansion to kill Stella?" Amber asked around a bite of pink lemonade cupcake.

"She says she grabbed the sword on her way out for her protection. Either way, she's looking at some heavy persecution for what she did with the body."

Amber and I both leaned in to hear more.

"Roberta had gone out the back entrance by this time. Dorothy claims that Stella charged toward her, and so she held out the sword in defense. Stella was impaled in the stomach. Dorothy tried to talk circles around the situation, but the next part is where Cliff came in, so I have some clearer details."

"Such as…?" As usual, I wasn't very patient when it came to learning the details and motivations of an investigation.

"Dorothy phoned Cliff from the Montrose mansion. We'll be able to check the phone records to confirm that call. She told him that Ben had gotten a new carpet and it was made of rabbit hide. She knew this would bother Cliff because Boots had once killed one of Cliff's well-loved rabbits. She told him to get over there and help her throw the carpet in with the tiger. By the time he got over there, she had rolled Stella

into the carpet she'd bled out on in the entry-
way."

"So she was already dead?" Amber asked.

"I believe so."

"And the carpet was not made of rabbit
hide?"

Alex shook his head. "Dorothy used that as
the excuse of why it had been so heavy, though.
Cliff is beating himself up pretty badly for believing her."

"So Dorothy Gallagher is responsible," I confirmed. "But why was Cliff out there with his
gun? Was he so angry about the rabbit hide carpet that he wanted to shoot Boots?"

Alex shook his head. "Dorothy told Cliff to
go home quickly before Ben got home, but when
Cliff heard the tiger going crazy, he couldn't help
but go over and see why. When he caught sight of
a woman, still partially wrapped in the carpet, he
ran for his gun to try and save her."

"Dorothy is the one who should have
checked herself in at the psych ward," Amber
said. "Cliff seems like he was just too trusting."

"Dorothy probably needed some help to get
through the grief over her husband." I always
had a habit of seeing a person's pain, even if
they had killed someone. "Not that it's any kind
of excuse, but grief can really overtake a person.
You're right," I said to Amber. "She needs professional help."

I was just glad I had Alex and Amber, and

even Hunch. Without them, who knew how much I'd still be struggling with my own grief.

"Who wants another cupcake?" I asked.

Alex and Amber both held up their empty plates, their smiles telling me that they were ready to move on to brighter days.

THE END

Up Next: Murder During the Antique Auction

Some people will kill for the perfect antique. The question is… who did?

When Mallory and Amber try their hand at catering their first event—an antique auction held on New Year's Eve—they have high hopes for helping the locals ring in the new year with a little bit of culinary decadence. But when a highly anticipated collector fails to bid on a piece he'd been prattling on about for most of a year, the antique dealer is sure something is wrong.

Has the collector only gone missing? Or was someone willing to literally kill him to get their hands on a prized antique?

Join My Cozy Mystery Readers' Newsletter Today!

Would you like to be among the first to hear about new releases and sales, and receive special excerpts and behind-the-scene bonuses?

Sign up now to get your free copy of *Mystery of the Secret Ingredients – A Mallory Beck Cozy Holiday Mystery,* where Amber enters a cooking competition and Mallory puts aside her own nagging mystery in order to help her.

You'll also get access to special epilogues to accompany this series—an exclusive bonus for newsletter subscribers. Sign up below and receive your free mystery:

https://www.subscribepage.com/ mysteryreaders

From Mallory's
Recipe Box…

Dear Chad,

Here is the recipe you asked for. It's one of my favorites, so I'm glad you enjoyed it too. It was first shared with me by a French chef visiting my culinary school. Let me know when you make it and how it turns out for you, and maybe we can talk more on New Year's Eve, if you're still interested in having me and Amber provide some sweet treats. Let's talk when you have a minute, but for now…enjoy!

Mallory

Salted Rum Caramel Tartlets
INGREDIENTS:
Chocolate-Chip Cookie Crust
1 cup + 2 tablespoons of all-purpose flour
1/2 teaspoon baking soda
1/2 teaspoon salt

1 stick unsalted butter, softened
1/2 cup brown sugar
1 teaspoon vanilla extract
1 egg
3/4 cup semi-sweet chocolate chips

Salted Rum Caramel
2 cups granulated sugar
1 cup heavy cream
1 stick unsalted butter (cut into chunks)
2 tablespoons rum (or a couple of drops of
rum extract and an extra tablespoon of butter)
2 vanilla beans, split lengthwise and seeds
scraped
pinch of sea salt

Ganache
1/2 cup heavy cream
3 1/2 ounces of dark chocolate, finely
chopped

Meringue
4 large egg whites, room temperature
pinch of cream of tartar
6 tablespoons sugar

INSTRUCTIONS:
To make the tartlet cookie dough, preheat the
oven to 350 degrees F. Using a nonstick muffin
pan is recommended, as this recipe can be a bit

messy.

1. Combine the flour, baking soda, and salt in a small bowl. Beat the butter, brown sugar, and vanilla extract in large mixer bowl until creamy (3 to 5 minutes). Add the eggs and beat well. Gradually beat in the flour mixture. Stir in the chocolate chips.

2. Press the cookie dough into the bottom and sides of 8-10 sections of the muffin pan. Bake for 8-10 minutes or until lightly golden on top.

3. Meanwhile, make the caramel. In a large deep heavy skillet, cook the sugar over moderately high heat, stirring constantly with a heatproof rubber spatula until the sugar is melted and turns a deep golden caramel. Remove the skillet from the heat, and add the chunks of butter one by one. Whisk until combined. The caramel will bubble. Slowly add the cream and then whisk until combined.

4. Return the pot to the heat and cook the mixture over moderate heat, stirring until the caramel has thickened (5-10 minutes). Remove from the heat, add rum and vanilla bean seeds, and a pinch of salt.

5. Once the cookie is done baking, slowly pour the caramel over the cookie, spreading it out as needed. This part may be messy! Let

the tart stand until the caramel is set (about 45 minutes).

6.   To make the ganache, place the chocolate in a heatproof bowl. In a small saucepan, bring cream to a boil. Pour the hot cream over the chocolate, and let stand for 2 minutes, then stir with a rubber spatula until smooth. Pour the ganache over the set tarts while the ganache is still warm. Let the tarts sit for at least 1 hour in the fridge before serving.

7.   Just before serving, make the meringue. Using an electric mixer, beat egg whites in medium bowl until frothy. Beat in cream of tartar. With mixer running, gradually add sugar. Beat until stiff peaks form. Spoon meringue over the tart. Using a kitchen torch, toast the meringue until golden in spots or place tarts under the broiler for less than one minute.

8.   Serve and enjoy!

Reviews matter...

Honest reviews help bring new books to the attention of other readers. If you enjoyed this book, I would be grateful if you would take five minutes to write a couple of sentences about it. You can find all the books in this series to leave reviews at the below link.

https://bit.ly/MalloryBeck

Thank you!

Mallory Beck Cozy Culinary Capers

Humorous and heartwarming cozy mysteries you won't soon forget.

Strong friendships and a cranky crime-solving cat who thinks he's a dog will keep you laughing out loud and turning the pages in this new whodunit. Along with plot twists and turns and suspense, you'll feel like you're spending time with old friends with this diverse group of characters tugging at your heart strings.

Snuggle up with a warm blanket and enjoy a little paw-on help in solving these small-town murder mysteries today!

Murder At Mile Marker 18

Murder At The Church Picnic

Murder At The Town Hall

Murder In The Vineyard

Murder At The Montrose Mansion

Murder At The Antique Auction

Acknowledgements

Thank you to my amazing team of advance readers, brainstormers, and supporters. I can't thank you enough for helping to get my little books a little notice in the huge and cluttered landscape of new releasing books. And to you, Reader: I appreciate you just for picking up this book and giving it a chance!

Thank you to my developmental editor, Louise Bates, my copyeditor, Sara Burgess, my "Strange Facts Expert" Danielle Lucas, my cover designer, Steven Novak, and illustrator, Ethan Heyde.

Special thanks to the book bloggers and book-stagrammers who have shared about my books, and for anyone who has taken the time to share them with their own social media following.

Thank you for joining me, along with Mallory, Amber, Alex, and Hunch on this journey. We're thrilled to have you along on this ride!

About The Author

Denise Jaden

Denise Jaden is a co-author of the
Rosa Reed Mystery Series by Lee
Strauss, the author of several crit-
ically-acclaimed young adult
novels, as well as the author of
several nonfiction books for
writers, including the
NaNoWriMo-popular guide Fast
Fiction. Her new Mallory Beck Cozy Culinary Mys-
tery Series will continue to launch throughout the
year.

In her spare time, she homeschools her son (a
budding filmmaker), acts in TV and movies, and
dances with a Polynesian dance troupe. She lives
just outside Vancouver, British Columbia, with her
husband, son, and one very spoiled cat.

Sign up on Denise's website to receive bonus con-
tent as well as updates on her new Cozy Mystery
Series. Find out more at www.denisejaden.com

JAN 1 0 2023

Made in the USA
Las Vegas, NV
27 April 2022